A SEASON OF SECRETS
AMISH BONNET SISTERS: LEGACY OF FAITH
BOOK TWO

SAMANTHA PRICE

Copyright © 2025 by Samantha Price

All rights reserved.

No part of this book may be reproduced in any form or by any electronic or mechanical means, including information storage and retrieval systems, without written permission from the author, except for the use of brief quotations in a book review.

CHAPTER 1

Chess ran, his breath ragged, his legs aching. He hadn't stopped since the flames began to spread, curling hungrily up the walls of his grandmother's shop. The smell of burning sawdust clung to his clothes, his skin, even his hair. He could still hear the crackle of the fire in his ears, even as he stumbled across fields under the cover of night.

The world was quiet now.

Too quiet.

The darkness swallowed him as he ran—fields blending into forests, dirt paths turning into nothing but a blur beneath his feet. The fire wasn't his fault. Not really. But that didn't matter. No one would see it that way, not after the car. Not after everything else he'd done.

His father would rage, his mother would cry, and everyone in town—Amish or not—would whisper about him. *Chess Braithwaite*, the troublemaker. The one who crashed a stolen car into his grandmother's shop. The one who set the place on fire.

He wiped sweat from his forehead with a shaky hand. His legs burned, and his lungs felt like they'd been scraped raw.

He didn't even know where he was going at first, not until Jared's name popped into his mind.

Jared was different. He wouldn't turn him in. He wouldn't hate him like everyone else.

The thought pulled Chess forward, his direction finally clear. He didn't know Jared all that well, but what little he did know told him that Jared would keep quiet. Jared didn't judge people—he wasn't like the others.

By the time Chess saw the faint outline of Jared's house through the trees, he was beyond exhaustion. Sweat had dried to a chill against his skin, and his shoes were caked in mud.

The small barn next to the house loomed like a shadow, the doors left slightly ajar. Chess let out a breath of relief. He'd made it. Slipping inside the barn, he bent over, hands on his knees, trying to catch his breath.

It smelled like hay and animals, better than smoke, though the fire still clung to him like a curse. He swallowed hard, taking in his surroundings.

The barn was quiet except for the soft snuffling of horses. Chess climbed the wooden ladder to the loft, hauling himself up with weak arms.

The loft was empty, just old hay bales and a thick layer of dust that made his nose itch. He sank into the hay, his chest still heaving. The darkness here felt safer somehow, even if his thoughts wouldn't let him rest.

The fire had started so fast. One second, everything was fine, and the next, flames were licking up the walls. *It must've been the candle.*

He'd been so careful at first, lighting it when he sat there with his cat, needing the warmth as the evening air turned cold. He rubbed his face hard, guilt clawing at him.

Stupid.

What would his father say? What would Iris think? And his grandmother—*Don't think about that.*

Don't think about the shop.

It would've been burnt to the ground by now. Chess couldn't go home now. He'd already caused too much trouble.

First crashing the car, now this. The police would think he'd done it on purpose. *Arson,* that's what they'd call it. And once that word was out there, it wouldn't matter if it was true or not.

He curled up tighter in the hay, wrapping his arms around his knees. The loft was freezing, the night air creeping in through cracks in the wood, but he didn't care.

He couldn't sleep anyway. Every time he closed his eyes, he saw the flames again.

They're going to hate me.

CHAPTER 2

Iris was getting ready for bed when an orange glow out the window caught her eye. She stuck her head out the open window and saw flames shooting up from the shop.

"Grandma!" she screamed, already racing for the stairs. "Fire! The shop's on fire!"

She burst through the front door into the cool night air, her heart pounding.

A familiar meow made her look down—Romeo was running toward her from the direction of the shop, his tail puffed up in distress. She scooped him up and hugged him to herself. There was only one way Romeo would be so far from home.

Please, she prayed, *please don't let Chess be behind this.*

"Fire!" Iris screamed again, her voice raw with panic. "Fire!" Romeo leaped out of her arms. She grabbed him before he went too far and hurried to put him in the house. As she did so, she yelled as loudly as she could. "Grandma, wake up!"

Wilma hurried down the stairs, tying her shawl over her shoulders. "Did you say fire?"

"Yes." Iris ran back outside and Wilma followed.

Wilma froze at the sight of the blaze, her mouth opening slightly.

The house door banged open behind them, and Matthew appeared.

"What happened?" Matthew barked, but Iris could barely respond. Her voice had caught in her throat.

"The shop—it's burning. I—I don't know how."

Matthew didn't hesitate. "Iris, call the fire department. Now."

"What? I—"

"The barn phone," he snapped, pointing toward the barn. "Go!"

She spun on her heel, her shoes slipping in the dirt as she bolted for the barn. Behind her, Matthew had already grabbed the first thing he saw—two heavy burlap sacks lying by the side of the house.

Iris darted into the barn, her hands shaking as she fumbled in the dark for the phone. She knew it was here somewhere—on a small table near the feed bins. Her fingers finally closed around the cold receiver, and she pressed the phone to her ear, trying to steady her breathing. "Come on, come on," she muttered as the line clicked and the ringing began.

"911, what is your emergency?" a calm voice answered.

"There's a fire!" Iris blurted, the words tumbling over themselves. "It's at my grandmother's shop—our property! Please, you have to hurry!"

"Stay calm, miss. What's the address?"

She rattled off the location, her voice breaking. "It's bad—it's spreading fast!"

"Fire crews are on their way," the voice assured her. "Stay clear of the fire and make sure everyone is safe."

Iris hung up with trembling fingers and turned back to the open barn door. She could see the flames glowing brighter now, illuminating the trees and the outline of the shop. It was a disaster.

When she reached the yard, she saw Matthew darting dangerously close to the flames. He swung the soaked burlap sacks at the fire, trying to beat back the flames. Sparks shot up into the night, tiny embers floating in the air like fireflies.

"Matthew!" Iris screamed, horrified at how close he was. "Get back!"

He didn't stop.

She turned toward the house, where her grandmother still stood on the porch, frozen as though rooted to the spot. Her face was pale, her hands gripping her shawl tightly at her chest. "There's nothing we can do."

Wilma didn't move, her wide eyes reflecting the fire's glow. "The shop," she whispered

Iris grabbed her grandmother's arm. "It's not gone yet. The fire department is coming. Matthew's trying to stop it."

At the mention of his name, Wilma seemed to snap out of her daze. She blinked, her focus shifting from the blaze to Matthew's figure, barely visible now through the thick smoke. "What is that boy doing?" Wilma rasped, her voice shaky.

"He's trying to stop it."

As they stood together, helpless, the fire roared louder, the wooden beams inside the shop cracking and collapsing one by one. The smell of smoke filled the air, sharp and choking. Wilma coughed, and Iris quickly guided her farther back, closer to the safety of the house.

The minutes stretched on like hours. Iris wrapped an arm around her grandmother's shoulders, holding her close, but her eyes never left Matthew. He was relentless, swinging the makeshift firebreaks again and again. Sweat soaked his shirt, and ash streaked his face, but he didn't falter.

Finally, in the distance, Iris heard it—a siren. Relief swept through her, but the fire still blazed, and Matthew hadn't retreated yet.

"Matthew!" she yelled again, her voice hoarse. "They're coming. You don't have to do this anymore."

Whether he heard her or not, she couldn't tell, but slowly he began backing away, dropping the scorched burlap sacks to the ground. By the time the fire trucks arrived, red and white lights flashing across the property, Matthew had returned to where Iris and Wilma stood.

He was breathing hard, sweat dripping from his chin, but his expression was steady as he wiped soot from his brow.

"Are you both okay?" he asked gruffly, his eyes scanning the two of them.

Wilma nodded faintly, though she seemed too overwhelmed to speak.

Iris looked up at him, wide-eyed and shaken. "You—you were crazy to get that close."

"I had to try. Sorry, Wilma, we've lost most of it."

"As long as no one was hurt," Wilma said. "And thank you for what you did."

Iris gazed up at him. "That was truly heroic."

Matthew glanced at her and gave her half a smile then looked back at the scene.

The firefighters poured out of the trucks, shouting instructions to each other as they unrolled hoses and started tackling the flames. Iris watched in stunned silence as water blasted the fire, steam billowing up into the night air.

"It's under control now," Matthew said, more to himself than anyone else.

Iris turned to him, her chest still heaving. "How did this happen? Why would the shop just...?"

Matthew shook his head, his brow furrowing as he looked toward the blaze. "I don't know. But I think someone was in there tonight."

"What?" Iris asked sharply.

"Before I went to bed, I thought I saw a light down there. I looked harder and then the light had gone." His eyes narrowed, as if he was replaying the image in his mind. "I thought I was imagining it, but now I'm not so sure. If anyone was there, they're long gone by now."

Iris's heart sank. Chess had been hanging around the shop a lot lately, repairing it after he'd run into it with his father's car. He'd been restless, angry, acting out in ways no one understood.

"Chess," she whispered under her breath.

"What did you say?" Matthew asked.

"Nothing," Iris said quickly, shaking her head. "It doesn't matter right now."

Matthew gave her a searching look but didn't press the issue.

The firefighters working methodically to drown every last

ember. Wilma sat on the porch steps, her face buried in her hands. The shop—her husband's old shop, the place where so many memories were made—was gone.

Iris looked at Matthew, his face streaked with ash and exhaustion, and knew they'd all remember this night for a long time.

But as the smoke cleared, Iris's thoughts were already elsewhere—on Chess. She couldn't shake the nagging feeling that he'd been there.

And if he had, where was he now?

CHAPTER 3

Through the haze of smoke, a pair of headlights cut through the darkness. Florence and Carter pulled up quickly, parking behind the fire trucks. The door on the driver's side flew open, and Florence stepped out. Carter followed, his face lined with concern as he took in the smoldering remains of the shop.

"What's happened?" Florence called as she hurried toward them.

Wilma was now seated on the steps of the house, a firefighter crouched beside her, but it was Iris who spotted her parents first. She ran toward them.

"Mom, Dad!" she cried. "Where's Chess?"

Florence frowned, blinking at her daughter. "Chess? He's at home—sleeping. We saw the smoke from our place."

"Did you *see* him at home?" Iris persisted.

Carter's brow furrowed. "No. Why?"

"Because I think Chess might've been in there!" Iris's voice broke as she pointed to the shop.

Florence took a sharp breath, her expression faltering. "What? What makes you say that?"

Iris wiped a hand over her face, trying to steady herself. "Because of Romeo. He's here. I just put him inside the house. If Romeo's here, there's only one way he could've gotten here."

Florence stilled, her face paling.

Carter's gaze snapped toward the house, his mouth tightening. "That can't be right. Romeo never leaves the house. Ever."

"I know," Iris said, her voice rising. "But he's here, Mom. He's here, and Chess isn't."

For a moment, all three of them stood frozen.

"Let's go," Carter said suddenly, grabbing Florence's arm and steering her back toward the car.

Florence looked over her shoulder as they climbed into the vehicle, her voice tight. "Stay here, Iris. We'll find him."

Iris stood rooted to the spot as their car reversed and sped down the gravel drive, its taillights disappearing into the dark.

At their house on the neighboring orchard, Carter flung open the front door, calling, "Chess!" His voice echoed through the empty halls as Florence rushed in behind him.

"Chess!" Florence yelled, running toward the staircase. She paused at the bottom, listening for any movement upstairs. Nothing.

Carter checked the living room first, his steps heavy with urgency. "He's not here!"

Florence hurried to Chess's room, throwing the door open. The bed was empty, the blankets tangled as if Chess hadn't slept there at all. She scanned the room quickly.

Carter appeared in the doorway. "Anything?"

"No." Florence's shoulders sagged as she stared at the bed. "He's not here. Anywhere."

Carter ran a hand through his hair. "I don't think he's run away. There's no note."

Florence frowned at her husband. "A note? What makes you think he'd leave a note? That would require thought and planning, Carter. Not exactly Chess's strong suit."

Carter sighed, nodding reluctantly. "Sadly, that's true."

They stood in silence for a moment, the realization settling over them like a weight. Chess wasn't here. And that meant only one thing, and it wasn't good.

Florence turned to Carter. "We need to go back to Wilma's."

Carter didn't argue. "Let's go." He grabbed the car keys.

When they pulled up at Wilma's house for the second time that night, the fire trucks were preparing to leave. Matthew stood by the house, his face streaked with soot, speaking quietly with a firefighter. Iris was pacing on the porch, her arms wrapped tightly around herself.

Iris looked up when she heard the car and ran to her parents. "Did you find him?"

Florence stepped out slowly, shaking her head. "He's not there, Iris."

"What do you mean?"

Carter slammed the car door shut, his expression grim. "We looked everywhere—his room, the living room, the barn—he's not at home."

"He's really missing?" Iris's voice trembled.

Florence nodded slowly. "Yes. He's gone."

Matthew raised his hands to try to calm everyone. "Hey, no one was in there. If he was there, he's long gone."

Florence heaved a sigh of relief. "Are you sure, Matthew?"

"I am."

"It's all my fault," Iris said with a whine.

Carter stepped closer, his voice firm but gentle. "This isn't your fault, Iris. Chess makes his own choices."

Wilma, still sitting quietly on the steps, looked up at them with wide, tired eyes. "Did I hear someone say Chess is missing?"

"Yes," Florence said softly, her voice shaking for the first time. "We thought he was at home, but he's not. Matthew said no one was harmed in the fire, so that's something."

"No, but he probably started the fire," Iris blurted out.

Wilma's shoulders slumped. "This is not good," she murmured.

The group stood in silence, the smoldering remains of the shop crackling faintly in the distance. Florence put a hand on Carter's arm, her voice barely above a whisper. "Where would he go?"

Carter shook his head. "I don't know, but don't worry he won't go far."

"Where do we even start?" Iris asked.

CHAPTER 4

Morning came with the faint sounds of movement outside. Chess heard the creak of the barn doors, the soft voices of Jared's mother, Debbie, and her husband, Gabe. He peeked through the cracks in the loft floorboards, just enough to see them loading a buggy with baskets and crates. They must've been heading to market, where Debbie had her tea stall.

He stayed still, barely breathing, until their horse and buggy rattled down the dirt road and disappeared into the trees. When all was quiet again, Chess climbed down from the loft. His entire body felt heavy, like he'd aged twenty years overnight.

He hesitated before walking to the house. What if Jared wasn't alone? What if he was wrong about this whole thing and Jared wouldn't be on his side?

But he didn't have anywhere else to go.

Chess pushed the back door open and stepped inside. The

kitchen smelled like fresh bread and coffee, the kind of calm, warm scent that made him miss home. Jared was sitting at the table, halfway through a plate of eggs and toast.

Jared's fork paused mid-air when he saw Chess. "Don't you knock?"

Chess froze in the doorway, unsure what to say. He must've looked awful—dirty, pale, and wrung out like an old dish towel.

Jared set his fork down, his expression shifting from shock to concern. "Hey… what's wrong?"

The words were like a dam breaking. Chess's vision blurred, and before he could stop himself, tears spilled over. His shoulders shook as he stumbled forward, collapsing into the nearest chair.

"I ran away," Chess choked out between sobs, covering his face with his hands. "I didn't know what to do. I was hiding in my grandmother's shop last night—with my cat—and a fire started."

Jared's chair scraped against the floor as he got up and came closer. "What?"

Chess wiped his face with his sleeve, trying to breathe, but the words kept spilling out. "I think the candle fell over or something. I don't know. I don't even remember knocking it. I saw the flames, and I just ran. I didn't know what to do, Jared. I panicked. I ran and ran."

Jared crouched beside him, his voice steady and calm. "You're saying the shop caught fire?"

Chess nodded miserably. "It's all my fault. They're going to hate me. Everyone already does."

"Hey," Jared said softly, resting a hand on Chess's arm. "Slow down. It was an accident, right?"

"Yeah, but nobody will believe that. Not after I crashed the car. I can't go home. I can't face anyone. I've run away."

Jared was quiet for a moment, his thoughtful expression unreadable. Then he stood, grabbed the kettle off the stove, and set it on to boil. "You hungry?" he asked casually.

Chess blinked up at him, confused. "What?"

"You want some breakfast?" Jared asked like it was just any other day. "Eggs, toast... I think there's jam left."

Chess hesitated, his stomach growling despite himself. "I guess."

Jared nodded, turning back to the stove. "You can stay here, you know. As long as you need. I won't tell anyone."

Chess stared at him. "Really?"

Jared glanced over his shoulder, a small smile on his face. "Yeah. You're safe here."

"But... what if someone comes looking for me?"

"Stay in the loft in the barn. I can make you a bed up there—some blankets, a pillow. It won't be much, but it's better than nothing."

Chess's throat tightened again, but this time it wasn't from fear. It was relief. "Thanks."

Jared waved him off as if it were no big deal. "You'd do the same for me. Not that you'd ever need to."

Chess wasn't sure that was true, but he didn't argue. He let the warmth of Jared's words sink in, softening the hard knot of guilt in his chest.

"You're sure I can stay?" Chess asked, just to hear it again.

"As long as you need," he said firmly. "We'll figure it out." Jared brought a plate over to the table and set it down in front of him.

Chess picked up a piece of toast, his hands still shaking. He didn't know what would happen next—whether the police would charge him for arson or whether his family would ever forgive him—but for now he wasn't running.

CHAPTER 5

Back at Wilma's place, the firefighters had left behind little more than a charred skeleton of what used to be Wilma's shop. Smoke still curled lazily into the dark sky, the smell of it lingering thick and heavy, settling into everything like a bad memory.

Matthew stood near the scorched remains, his hands on his hips, staring down at the blackened rubble. He crouched, brushing away a thin layer of soot with his hand. There, half-burned but unmistakable, was a can of cat food.

Matthew picked it up, turning it over. Part of the label was gone, but the rest was clear as day. He frowned, turning to face the others who had gathered nearby: Florence, Carter, Iris, and Wilma, who still stood in her shawl, wringing it tightly in her hands. "Look at this," he held up the can. "I found this in the ashes here—a can of cat food."

Iris's breath hitched. "Romeo's food?"

"Has to be," Matthew said, standing straight. "We can

assume Chess was here last tonight. I don't know why, but he must've brought the cat with him. He left this behind."

Florence exchanged a worried glance with Carter. "Where do you think he went?"

"I don't know," Matthew admitted. "But let's give Chess a few hours to come back before we panic. He's probably scared out of his wits right now."

"I agree," Carter said with a nod. "Especially with all the trouble he's been in lately."

"That's what I'm worried about. What if he doesn't come back at all?" Florence clung onto Carter's arm, staring up at him.

"We'll give him a day. If no one's heard from him, I'll organize a search," Carter replied.

"I'll help. I'll get all the men organized and ready to go," Matthew offered.

"I appreciate that, Matthew."

Wilma put her arm around Florence. "I'm sure he'll be back."

"I hope so." Florence sniffed.

"Wilma, the community will do a fundraiser to help you rebuild this. That's what we did when the Millers' barn burned down."

"No," Wilma said. "It's not necessary. It's not like a barn, and we weren't using it."

"If funds are needed, then I'll fix things. No need to involve the community," Carter said.

Matthew gave a nod. "There's nothing anyone can do now. Get some sleep if you can. I'll keep an eye out and if I see Chess, I'll tell him to head back home."

"Thanks, Matthew." Carter clasped his shoulder in appreciation.

Florence and Carter hugged Iris goodbye before heading back to their car. Wilma gave Iris a quick embrace, then started toward the house. A soft meow caught Iris's attention, and she spotted Romeo peering through the window. She hurried over to scoop him up.

"Let's get him something to eat," Wilma said, leading the way inside. She set out a bowl of food and water for him near the back door.

After that, Iris sank onto the couch, her legs giving out beneath her. Her hands rubbed restlessly at her knees, guilt and unease written all over her face.

Wilma lingered near the stairs, looking back at Iris with weary eyes. "Are you going to try and get some sleep?"

Iris nodded faintly. "In a little while."

Satisfied, Wilma turned, her movements slow and heavy with the weight of the night. As she climbed the stairs, her voice drifted back down. "Do try and get some rest and don't worry about your brother."

"I won't," Iris replied softly.

The house fell silent again, until Matthew walked in and pulled a chair closer to where Iris sat. He dropped into it with a sigh, his strong hands hanging loosely between his knees. "You okay?" he asked after a moment.

Iris hesitated, staring at nothing in particular. "Yeah," she lied, then shook her head. "No. Not really. I'm sorry, Matthew. About everything. About the shop…"

Matthew frowned. "What are you apologizing for?"

"Because it's gone," she said, her voice cracking. "And you—

you were trying to help Chess fix it after he wrecked it the first time. I know you put so much work into it."

"Don't worry about that," Matthew said gently. "It's just a building. I can build another one if I have to."

Iris looked up at him, her eyes glassy with tears she was too stubborn to shed. "It's more than a building. It was hers—Grandma's. And I don't know what Chess was doing there or why he ran, but…" She trailed off, biting her lip to keep it from trembling.

Matthew leaned forward, his elbows resting on his knees. "I'm sure he didn't mean for this to happen. I know it. He's really a good kid."

"I hope you're right," Iris murmured, running her hands over her face. She exhaled slowly, trying to settle herself, when a soft thump broke the silence.

Romeo leapt onto the couch, landing beside her. The cat rubbed his face against her arm before curling up in her lap like he belonged there. Iris let out a shaky laugh, her fingers stroking through the cat's fur.

Matthew watched her, his expression softening. "Are you going to try to get some sleep?"

"No. I won't be able to sleep and besides it's daytime now. I'm too stirred up. I keep thinking about Chess. Where he is. If he's okay. If I…"

Matthew shook his head. "Don't go blaming yourself for this."

"I could've stopped him," she said softly. "I knew something wasn't right when I saw Romeo, but I guess it was too late by then."

Matthew stood, stretching his arms, and then sat back

down, leaning comfortably into the chair. "I'll sit with you for a while."

Iris glanced at him, surprised. "You don't have to do that."

"I know," he said simply, settling in. "But I will."

"Thank you," Iris said finally.

Matthew looked at her. "Don't mention it."

Romeo shifted in her lap, his purring growing louder. "Let's talk about something else. I need to calm down a bit."

"Okay. What would you like to talk about?" Matthew asked.

Iris thought for a moment. "How did you feel seeing Grace again?"

He grinned. "That's a shift in topics for sure."

"Well?"

"I'm not sure if I want or need to talk about that. Doesn't seem important after the fire."

"I know, but talking calms me down and I can't think of anything else to talk about."

"Okay. Well… It was different. I think she felt worse than I did. Until Daniel walked her outside. I don't know why he did that. It was a bit weird."

"Maybe it's time you looked for someone else."

"Yeah, well, it's not that easy." He sniffed his shirt. "I need to shower and change my clothes. I smell like smoke."

"Everything does now, thanks to Chess," Iris stood up, still holding Romeo. "I'll see you later today. I'm going up to my room."

"You okay now?"

"I'll be fine. Thanks for sitting with me Matthew. What will you do now?"

"I'm going to work. Fairfax, the boss, needs a lot of help

now leading up to harvest. I'll get a few hours in and come back and get some breakfast."

"Let me know when you get back, and I'll make it for you. Pancakes is your favorite, right?"

He grinned. "Yeah. Thanks, Iris."

"It's the least I could do for a hero."

Matthew burst out laughing. "I'm not a hero."

"I think you are. You didn't hesitate when you saw the fire. You didn't even think about your own safety. You're a hero."

He shook his head. "I'm not, but you can think that if you want."

Iris gave him a smile, and took Romeo upstairs with her.

CHAPTER 6

After breakfast, Jared had insisted Chess do chores while he was hiding out.

Chess wiped sweat from his brow with the back of his hand, glaring down at the rake in his grip. His arms ached, and his back was starting to throb from the repetitive motion of spreading hay evenly across the barn floor.

"Why do I have to do this?" he groaned, his voice echoing in the barn. He dropped the rake with a clatter, leaning against one of the beams for support.

Jared, who was stacking bales of hay in the corner, barely looked up. "Because chores don't do themselves, Chess. You've got to learn how to do these things anyway."

"I thought chores were supposed to be fun or something," Chess muttered, kicking at a stray clump of hay with his boot. "Anyway, I'm hiding, remember? Why do I have to do chores while I'm hiding?"

Jared stopped what he was doing and leaned against the

stack of hay bales. "Because you're not a stray cat hiding in the barn for a free pass. You're staying here, and if you're staying here, you help out. It doesn't matter if you're hiding or not. Do the chores, get them out of the way, and then we'll do something fun. That sound like a good idea?"

Chess crossed his arms, narrowing his eyes. "Fun. Yeah, like what? What's so fun about this place?"

Jared's lips twitched in the faintest hint of a smile. "We could build a birdhouse."

Chess blinked. "A birdhouse? That's your idea of having a good time?"

"It is when you make them as well as I do," Jared replied, pushing himself off the haystack. "It's my job. I sell them at the markets."

Chess's brow furrowed. "Yeah, I heard that you do that, but do you really make money doing that?"

Jared nodded. "Yeah. I've made enough. Enough to move out of here, if I wanted to."

"Then why don't you?" Chess asked, genuinely curious.

Jared picked up the rake Chess had abandoned and began tidying up the stray hay. "Because I like being around family. I don't want to live on my own."

Chess snorted. "I'd love to be on my own. My folks are way too harsh. There are way too many rules, and then there's Iris." he rolled his eyes. "Don't get me started about her."

Jared stopped raking, leaning on the handle as he studied Chess. "You might think being on your own would solve all your problems, but it's not as great as you'd think. No one to talk to. No one to have your back. And no one to help you when you mess up."

Chess shrugged. "I'd rather take my chances."

"Look, Chess, I get it. You're frustrated. But let me ask you something. Do you really want to end up like those guys you've been hanging around with? The ones who steal and get into trouble all the time? Yes, I've heard about them. News travels fast around our community, and your mother used to be one of us. I eventually hear about everything."

Chess tensed, avoiding Jared's gaze. "My friends are not all bad," he mumbled.

"They might seem cool now, but do you really want to end up in jail? Locked away, no fresh air, no sunlight on your face. You don't want that life, Chess. Trust me."

Chess hesitated, the image of bars and confined spaces flashing through his mind. He shook his head quickly. "No, I don't want that. But I'm bored, Jared. I can't just sit here doing chores all day."

"Then let's get these chores done so we can do something else," Jared said, his tone softening. "I'll show you how to build a birdhouse. Who knows? You might be good at it. Maybe even good enough to sell a few of your own."

Chess tilted his head. "You really think I could make money doing stuff like that?"

Jared grinned. "Only one way to find out."

Reluctantly, Chess picked up the rake and resumed moving the hay. It wasn't exactly fun, but he had to admit, Jared had a way of making him feel like he wasn't just wasting time.

A while later, with the chores finally done, Jared led Chess to a small workbench set up in the corner of the barn. Various tools and scraps of wood were neatly lined up in rows across the bench, and a nearly finished birdhouse sat on the edge. In front of them on a wall, tools were neatly lined up, each on their own hooks.

"This is where the creations happen," Jared said with a smile, gesturing to the bench. "Let's see if you've got any woodworking talents."

Chess approached the bench cautiously, eyeing the tools. "All right. I'll give anything a try once. So, what do I do?"

Jared handed him a piece of sandpaper. "Start by smoothing out this plank. You don't want any rough edges."

Chess took the sandpaper and started working, his movements awkward at first. "This feels... weird. Like I'm just scratching the wood."

"You'll get the hang of it," Jared said encouragingly. "Just keep at it."

As Chess sanded, Jared explained the process of building a birdhouse—measuring, cutting, assembling the pieces. Chess listened, occasionally nodding, but his focus stayed on the plank in front of him. Slowly but surely, the wood began to feel smoother under his hands.

Jared examined what he'd done. "Not bad. Now let's move on to the next step."

They worked side by side, Jared guiding Chess through each part of the process. By the time the birdhouse started to take shape, Chess felt a small sense of pride bubbling up. He wasn't sure if it was the work itself or the fact that someone was actually teaching him something useful for once.

"So, you really make enough money doing this to get by?" Chess asked as he hammered a nail into place.

Jared nodded. "Yeah, I already told you I do. It's not a

fortune, but it's enough. And it's honest work. That's what matters."

Chess thought about that, his hammer pausing. Honest work. With his family being so rich, he'd never had to worry about money before, but something told him his family wasn't just going to hand him money when the time came. His folks would make him 'work' for it in some way. It wasn't something he'd given much thought to before his car crash. But watching Jared, seeing the care he put into every detail, Chess started to wonder if maybe he could make it on his own when he got older—without his father's money.

"Maybe this hiding thing won't be so bad," Chess said, a small smile tugging at his lips.

Jared laughed. "Told you. Now let's finish this birdhouse. We've got a long day ahead of us tomorrow."

Chess stared at him. "Why? What's going on tomorrow?"

"Lots more chores," Jared said with a laugh.

Chess groaned.

CHAPTER 7

Wilma stood solemnly near the ashes, her arms crossed tightly over her chest. She looked up when she heard a horse and buggy approaching and was pleased to see Adaline in the driver's seat with Ada alongside.

They climbed down from the buggy and made their way toward Wilma.

"We heard about the fire," Ada said softly, her gaze sweeping over the blackened debris.

Ada shook her head, clicking her tongue in dismay. "They think Chess did this?"

Wilma nodded. "Yes. He's gone, no one can find him. He hasn't come back. They think it must've been him. We even think he might've been hiding out in here... and he also took Iris's cat. But we have Romeo now. He turned up just this morning, looking none the worse for wear."

"Seems like there's always something going on around here. But all this mess... who's going to clean it up?" Adaline asked.

Wilma sighed. "That's something I don't know yet. The man from the fire department said something about getting the police involved to see if it was arson. I told him no. There wasn't much value in the shop anyway. I'm taking it as a sign we should just let it go."

Ada stared at her friend. "Is that what you want, Wilma?"

"I'm not sure. Let's go inside," Wilma suggested quietly, leading them toward the house. Once inside, Wilma set about making tea, the familiar routine offering a small sense of normalcy amid the chaos.

Once they were gathered around the kitchen table, Iris joined them.

Ada broke the silence. "This fire... it's just one thing after another, isn't it?"

Wilma forced a smile. "Seems that way. And speaking of 'things,' how about our little matchmaking efforts?"

Ada groaned softly. "Don't remind me. Daniel was supposed to make Matthew jealous. Not actually go on a date with Grace."

Adaline burst into laughter. "That's what happens when you meddle!"

Iris, who had been quietly listening, found herself nodding in agreement. Though she remained silent, her heart twisted slightly at the mention of Matthew.

Adaline wasn't done. She leaned back in her chair, her grin mischievous. "But, I did think Matthew looked a little jealous."

Iris's heart gave an involuntary lurch, but she kept her expression neutral, focusing intently on her tea. She didn't want to give away even the smallest hint of how that comment affected her.

Trying to steer the conversation away from the uncomfortable flutter in her chest, Iris cleared her throat. "Maybe Daniel and Grace are suited for each other. Maybe they'll get married."

Ada chuckled, shaking her head. "Well, that would certainly be something. Grace doesn't seem the type to settle down quickly."

Wilma shrugged thoughtfully. "Stranger things have happened. People often find love where they least expect it."

"Well, I heard from Cherish that Grace and Daniel were going to go for a buggy ride sometime soon," Adaline said.

Wilma's eyebrows rose. "Is that so?"

Ada nodded. "Yes, she visited us last night."

Wilma glanced toward the window, her thoughts drifting back to Chess. The laughter faded, replaced by an uneasy silence. "Florence must be so worried about Chess."

Ada set down her cup, concern etching lines across her face. "What will you do if he doesn't come back today?"

Wilma exhaled a weary sigh, folding her hands on the table. "If he's not back by nightfall, we're going to organize a search party for tomorrow. That's the plan."

Adaline leaned forward. "A search party? Like, with everyone from the community?"

Wilma nodded. "Yes, as many as we can gather. I imagine they'll start early, cover the woods, fields, any places he might've gone. He can't have gotten far."

Iris stared into her tea. "Why does it always come to this with Chess?" she muttered softly, though not expecting an answer.

Ada said, "Because sometimes people lose their way, and it takes more than one person to help them find it again."

Wilma gave a small nod of agreement. "And no matter how much trouble he causes, he's still family. We don't give up on family until we've tried everything."

Adaline tilted her head thoughtfully. "Well, if we're searching tomorrow, I'm helping."

Ada shot her a look. "We'll see. It might not be safe. Leave it to the men."

"I can help," Adaline insisted, but Ada didn't respond, the conversation trailing off.

CHAPTER 8

That afternoon, Florence and Carter arrived at Wilma's place. She knew from their faces that there had been no sign of Chess. Behind her, Matthew lingered, arms crossed, while Iris sat on the worn armchair near the hearth, absentmindedly patting Romeo.

"No sign of Chess?" Wilma asked.

"No," Carter said with his head lowered.

"Come in," Wilma said quietly, stepping aside to let Florence and Carter enter.

"Matthew, you can help with the search party?" Carter asked.

Matthew straightened, his brow furrowed. "I'll organize it. I'll get everyone together." His voice carried a quiet authority, and Iris felt the familiar flutter in her chest despite the grim circumstances.

Carter shook his head vehemently. "We can't involve the

police. Not after the other incident. Chess has had enough trouble with them already."

Florence sighed, glancing at her husband. "Then what do *we* do? Do we join Matthew's search tomorrow? We can't just sit around doing nothing."

Carter rubbed his chin thoughtfully. "I'll hire a helicopter to comb the area. It'll cover more ground faster than we can on foot."

"But they won't know what Chess looks like," Florence pointed out.

"You and I can go up in the helicopter," Carter replied, already pulling out his phone to make arrangements.

"Good idea," Florence murmured, though her worry lines deepened.

"We can get tracking dogs too," Carter added. "Bloodhounds."

"Ah, great idea," Florence agreed.

"I'll get onto that now." Carter walked outside to make some calls.

Iris continued to stroke Romeo, her annoyance simmering just beneath the surface. Chess always seemed to be the center of attention, his reckless antics overshadowing everything. She had come here to spend a peaceful summer, to escape the dramas of her life back home, but instead, Chess had managed to drag her into his mess.

She glanced at Matthew, who was now deep in discussion with Florence about the logistics of the search party. His strong profile, the way his jaw tightened in determination, made her heart ache with a mix of admiration and something she didn't want to name. She hated that even now, in the midst of all this, her feelings for him were tangled up with her frustration over her brother.

Wilma noticed Iris's distant expression. "Iris, can you fetch some tea?"

Nodding, Iris rose, setting Romeo down. She moved to the kitchen, grateful for the brief reprieve from the heavy atmosphere. As she filled the kettle, her thoughts drifted back to the day she arrived, full of hope for a fresh start, eager to learn from her grandmother about a simpler, more grounded way of life.

Returning with the tea, she caught the tail end of Matthew's conversation.

"I'll go now and get the word out. We'll meet at dawn near the old mill. I'll get as many people as I can."

"That will be wonderful, Matthew." Florence accepted the tea with a nod of thanks, her hands trembling slightly. "Thank you, Iris."

Iris forced a small smile. "It's okay, Mamm."

As the evening wore on, plans were made, responsibilities assigned. Carter finalized the helicopter arrangement and the blood hounds, while Matthew outlined the ground search strategy.

After Florence and Carter left, Matthew lingered. He glanced at Iris, his gaze softening.

"You okay?" he asked quietly.

She looked up, surprised by the question. For a moment, she considered brushing it off with a simple "I'm fine," but something in his eyes made her pause. "I just wanted a summer without all this," she admitted softly. "Is that too much to ask?"

Matthew gave a small, understanding smile. "Sometimes the things we want most are the hardest to hold onto."

His words lingered and she had to wonder, was he talking about Grace? He stepped toward the door. "Where are you going?" Iris asked.

"I've got to drive around and get the word out about the search party."

"No one has phones in their barns like Grandma does?"

"Some but not all. Do you want to come in the buggy to keep my company?"

Iris looked over at her grandmother who gave her a nod. "You can if you want."

"Sure." Iris jumped to her feet.

CHAPTER 9

For Grace Wednesday took forever to arrive. This was the first date she'd gone on after Matthew. During their very much on again off again romance, she hadn't dated anyone.

Grace smoothed down her apron and peeked out the kitchen window, her pulse quickening as she spotted the black horse and buggy pulling up in the driveway. She could make out Daniel's broad shoulders as he guided the reins, his posture confident and easy. She turned back to Christina, who was busy fussing with a pot of coffee on the stove. "He's here," Grace said, trying to sound calm.

Christina glanced over her shoulder, her eyes twinkling. "Well, don't keep him waiting. He might change his mind."

Grace rolled her eyes, but a small smile tugged at her lips. She stepped outside just as Daniel climbed down from the buggy.

"Good morning," he said with a small, shy smile, tipping his hat. "Ready to go?"

"I suppose so," Grace replied, trying to mask her nerves. "Where are we headed?"

Daniel hesitated, a faint blush creeping up his neck. "Nowhere in particular. I thought we'd just take a drive and talk. Get to know each other better."

Grace tilted her head, studying him.

Daniel grinned and offered his hand to help her into the buggy. Once she was seated, he climbed up beside her, taking the reins. The buggy jolted slightly as the horse moved forward.

For a few minutes, they rode in companionable silence, the breeze cool but pleasant. Grace glanced at Daniel, who seemed focused on the road ahead.

"Have you heard about the fire at the Baker Apple Orchard?" she asked.

Daniel nodded, his expression turning serious. "Hard not to. News like that spreads fast around here. Awful thing to happen. I heard Wilma's old shop burned down."

"It did," Grace confirmed. "And they say Florence's son might've had something to do with it."

Daniel glanced at her, his brows knitting together. "Why would he do something like that?"

"I don't know," Grace admitted. "But you know how people talk. They're saying he's been acting out a lot lately, causing trouble. Maybe it was an accident, but..." She trailed off, unsure how to finish the thought.

Daniel shook his head. "Rumors can be dangerous, though. If it was an accident, folks should remember that. No need to make it worse for him."

Grace nodded, appreciating his measured response. "You're right. I suppose we'll find out the truth soon enough."

"There's a search party. I'm joining them later today."

"That's good of you."

"I should be there now, but I didn't want to break our date. I mean, we have a date and I wanted to keep it."

They fell quiet again, the conversation leaving a thoughtful pause between them. Daniel steered the buggy down a winding road, and Grace realized she didn't recognize the path they were taking.

"Where are we going?" she asked, glancing at him.

Daniel smiled. "Nowhere specific. Just driving. It's nice, isn't it? No rush, no destination. Just time to talk. And we can keep a lookout for Wilma's grandson while we do it."

"That's a good idea." Grace leaned back, letting herself relax. "It is nice. You're not what I expected, you know."

Daniel raised an eyebrow. "Oh? And what did you expect?"

Grace smirked. "Someone who'd plan a proper date, for one thing."

He laughed, the sound warm and unguarded. "Fair enough. I'll admit, I didn't put much thought into this. But I'll do better next time. At least I showed up. I mean, I thought about joining the search party."

"Well, you can take me home and join them if you want."

He looked over at her. "I wouldn't do that. I won't be responsible for disappointing a lady."

Grace was unable to hide her smile. "You're confident, I'll give you that."

"Not confident. Hopeful," he corrected.

They continued down the road, their conversation drifting

from topic to topic. Grace found herself laughing more than she expected, Daniel's easy humor and genuine curiosity putting her at ease.

He asked her about her favorite things, her family, and her thoughts on life in their community. In turn, she learned about his work, his siblings, and the mischief he used to get into as a boy. Then their conversation turned back to the fire at the Baker Apple Orchard.

"Why don't we swing past the orchard and take a look?" Daniel suggested.

"Sure, I'd like to see the damage. Is that odd that I'm curious?"

He laughed. "I hope not because I want to see too." He turned the horse and buggy around, took a left, and took the road to the Baker orchard.

The damage from the fire came into view. There were a few charred wooden posts sticking up and loads of rubble.

Grace leaned forward slightly, her heart sinking at the sight. "There's so little left. It's worse than I imagined."

"Fires like that don't leave much behind. It was a good thing the house didn't catch fire too."

"Oh, you're right. That would've been awful."

As they continued to take in the devastation, a loud creak pierced the quiet. The last post that was standing collapsing with a resounding crash.

"Oh no!" Grace exclaimed. "Do you think we caused that by saying awful things?"

Daniel clicked the reins, urging the horse forward at a brisk trot. "Let's get out of here before we cause something else to happen."

Grace covered her mouth with her hand, as she giggled. "Oh dear," she muttered. "I shouldn't laugh."

Daniel glanced over at her, his lips curving into a smile. "I was thinking the same thing. That's why I took off so fast."

Grace shook her head, trying to suppress another laugh. "You're something else, Daniel."

"I try."

"I'm surprised you stayed in the community," Grace said at one point. "It sounds from what you said before that you had your share of wild days."

Daniel shrugged. "I thought about leaving once or twice, but it never felt right. This life—the simplicity of it, the community—it's where I belong. What about you? Ever thought about leaving?"

Grace hesitated, her gaze dropping to her hands. "I did once. But my family needed me here, and I couldn't imagine leaving them. Besides, there's a lot of good here, too. It's not always easy, but it's home. I have two mothers now and two communities I can call home."

Daniel nodded, his expression thoughtful. "Home. That's a good way to put it."

The road curved, opening up to a wide stretch of farmland. Daniel slowed the buggy, letting the horse walk at a leisurely pace.

Grace took a deep breath, the fresh air filling her lungs. "It's beautiful out here," she said softly.

"It is," Daniel agreed. "Sometimes we get so caught up in our work, we forget to appreciate it."

She glanced at him. "Do you always talk like this on your driving dates? All deep and philosophical?"

Daniel laughed, shaking his head. "Not always. Just when I'm trying to impress someone."

Grace smirked. "Well, you get points for your effort."

They shared a smile, the moment lingering between them. Grace realized she felt... comfortable. More than that, she felt seen, in a way she hadn't expected. Daniel was so easy to talk with.

As they turned back toward town, Daniel broke the silence. "Next time, I'll pick a destination. Somewhere nice. A surprise."

"Next time?" Grace teased. "You're assuming a lot."

Daniel's grin was unabashed. "I'm optimistic."

Grace shook her head, but her smile betrayed her. "We'll see."

By the time they returned to Christina's house, Grace was hungry. Daniel hadn't even thought about getting them anything to eat. It was an odd kind of date.

Daniel helped her down from the buggy.

"Thank you for today," Grace said.

"Thank you," Daniel replied. "For giving me a chance."

She nodded, lingering for a moment before stepping back. "Bye, Daniel."

"Bye, Grace. Oh, and Grace?"

She turned to face him. "Yes?"

"How about we do this another time? Well, not this, but something else. What I'm saying is, will you come on another date with me?"

She loved how shy and awkward he sounded as though this really mattered to him. "I'd like that."

His face beamed with a smile, and Grace turned and walked into the house.

CHAPTER 10

Once Grace was inside the house, Christina greeted her with a curious look. "How was it?" she asked, leaning against the doorway.

Grace nodded. "It was good."

Christina raised an eyebrow. "Just good?"

"Yeah, we just drove around. And now I'm starving," Grace said, a faint grin tugging at her lips. "Didn't even stop for food."

Christina chuckled and gestured toward the kitchen. "The girls and I had soup for lunch. There's some left on the stove."

Grace followed her mother into the kitchen. Christina ladled out a bowl of soup and handed it to Grace, who sat at the table, the warmth of the bowl comforting in her hands.

"So," Christina pressed, sitting down across from her. "He didn't take you anywhere at all?"

Grace shook her head. "No. I don't know how he wasn't hungry. It's way past lunchtime."

Christina's eyes sparkled with mischief. "But do you like him?"

Grace hesitated, stirring her soup. "I think I do," she admitted. "But I'm not rushing in. He's such good company and we can talk and laugh so easily."

Christina nodded approvingly. "That's wise, not to jump into anything or rush."

Before Grace could take another bite, the twins burst into the kitchen, their eyes wide with curiosity.

"How was your date?" one of them blurted.

"Did he kiss you?" the other added, both of them giggling.

Grace rolled her eyes, trying to hide her amusement.

"Aren't you two supposed to be bringing in the washing?" Christina said.

The twins exchanged guilty looks. "We finished it," one protested.

Grace sighed, setting her spoon down. "Well, for your information, it was fine. And no, there was no kissing. Now go find something else to do before you get in trouble for bothering me."

The twins giggled again before scampering out of the room, leaving Grace shaking her head.

Christina laughed softly. "They mean well."

"They're impossible," Grace muttered with a smile.

CHAPTER 11

The soft creak of a buggy outside drew Wilma's attention away from the bloodhounds, which had just picked up Chess's scent and dashed into the orchard, their handler and an assistant close behind.

The afternoon sun hung high in the sky. Iris had gone for a walk hours ago and still hadn't returned. Now, Wilma's gaze shifted to the buggy as a young man stepped down—Daniel.

Wilma opened the door before he could knock, offering him a warm but curious smile. "Daniel, what brings you by?"

Daniel tipped his hat, his usual confidence dimmed by a flicker of unease in his eyes. "Afternoon, Wilma. I was hoping I could talk to you for a moment."

She stepped aside, gesturing for him to enter. "Come in. What's on your mind?"

He followed her into the living room and sat down, his posture stiff. Wilma could see the tension in his shoulders and the way his hands fidgeted with the brim of his hat.

"I'm sorry for the fire."

"Thank you. Worse than that is that Chess, my grandson is missing. The bloodhounds have the scent so hopefully they'll find him soon. I only hope he's alright. Anyway, I'm sure you didn't come about that."

"No, but I'm going to join the search party after this. I'm here about Grace. I… I'm not sure what I'm doing here. It's all going downhill. I've just come back from a date. She agreed to a second one, but I need guidance."

Wilma arched an eyebrow. "What do you mean?"

"I'm not good at dating. I thought you might have some good advice."

Wilma folded her hands in her lap, studying him carefully. "Why come to me about this? Can't you talk to your friends or your mother?"

He shook his head. "No. You're the one who set me up with Grace, so I figured you'd have some insight."

A low growl from his stomach made Daniel flush and press a hand to his abdomen.

Wilma's expression softened into a smile. "Hungry?" she asked.

He gave a sheepish grin. "A little."

"Come on," she said, rising from her chair. "I'll make you a sandwich. You can't think clearly on an empty stomach."

In the kitchen, Wilma moved with practiced ease, slicing bread and gathering ingredients. Daniel leaned against the counter, watching her.

"What did you do on your date?" she asked, glancing at him over her shoulder.

"Just drove around," he said. "Talked a little."

Wilma raised an eyebrow. "That's it?"

"I guess I didn't plan very well," he admitted. "I wasn't sure what she'd like."

"Well, you're lucky Grace is a kind girl," Wilma said, setting a plate with a sandwich in front of him. "But if you want my advice, put in a little more effort next time. Flowers, a nice picnic, maybe even a small gift. And don't forget to give her a genuine compliment. Girls like Grace notice the little things."

Daniel nodded, taking a bite of the sandwich. "I can do that," he said around a mouthful of food.

Wilma chuckled. "Slow down. There's more if you're still hungry. Oh, that sounds like a buggy." Wilma moved to the window and saw Ada and Adaline stepping down.

"Looks like you've got company. I'll leave you to it," Daniel said, finishing the last of his sandwich.

Wilma turned back to him with a smile. "You can stay if you like. Ada always has plenty to say, and she'd love to see you."

Daniel shook his head, standing and dusting crumbs from his hands. "I'd better go. Thanks for the advice, Wilma. And the sandwich."

She walked him to the door, watching as he climbed into his buggy and tipped his hat to Ada and Adaline before driving off. As the two women entered the house, Wilma couldn't help but feel a pang of guilt over Ada and her matchmaking. This was getting more complicated than she'd anticipated.

CHAPTER 12

It seemed like half the community had shown up to search for Chess. Soon they made their way to Debbie and Gabe's house where Chess had been hiding out, thanks to Jared.

Jared stood at the edge of his barn, arms crossed, as the group spread out, combing the surrounding area. Searchers moved through the fields and outbuildings. It was a close call when two men lingered near the barn, peering inside suspiciously before moving on.

Up in the loft, Chess crouched behind a pile of old hay bales, his heart pounding so loudly he was certain someone below would hear it. His palms were damp, and his breaths came shallow as he tried to steady himself. Jared had told him to hurry up there, to stay quiet, and Chess had done as he was told, dragging the ladder up behind him with trembling hands. Now, he huddled in the shadows, his eyes squeezed shut as if that would make him invisible.

He didn't want to be found. Not by the searchers, not by his family, not by the police. The thought of facing them—of seeing the disappointment in his parents' eyes or hearing the anger in Wilma's voice—was more than he could bear. And Jared... Jared would have to lie for him. Chess felt a stab of guilt at the thought. Jared didn't deserve to be dragged into his mess.

"Jared!" a voice called from outside, startling Chess. He clamped a hand over his mouth, forcing himself to stay still.

"Morning, Isaac," Jared replied. Chess heard the faint creak of the barn door as it swung open. "What can I do for you?"

"We're searching everywhere for Chess," Isaac said, his voice closer now. "You heard about the fire, right? And that he's missing?"

"Yeah, I heard," Jared said, his tone carefully neutral. "It's awful. I hope he's all right."

"Why haven't you joined the search then?"

"Not sure. Only just heard about it. I've got a ton of things to do.

"We all have. We're checking all the barns and outbuildings," Isaac continued. "Mind if we take a look around?"

Chess's stomach dropped. He pressed himself further into the corner, his fingers digging into the coarse hay. He could hear Jared's measured response, each word chosen with care.

"Of course," Jared said. "Take your time. I've got nothing to hide."

Chess's breath hitched. Jared wasn't lying, not exactly, but his words still sent a pang of unease through him. The sound of footsteps echoed below as Isaac and another man entered the barn. Chess strained his ears, catching snippets of their conversation as they moved around.

"Can't see anyone here," one of them said.

"What about the loft?" Isaac said, pointing upward.

Chess's heart stopped. He clenched his fists, willing himself to disappear. He felt the faint shift of the air as someone's gaze lingered on the ladder—or rather, where the ladder should have been.

"Doesn't look like there's a way up there," Jared said smoothly. "I took the ladder down weeks ago. Can't even tell you where it is. Haven't had a reason to go up myself."

"Makes sense," Isaac said, his tone distracted. "All right, let's move on. Thanks, Jared."

"No problem," Jared replied. "I hope you find him soon. He's probably scared out of his mind."

Chess felt a wave of relief wash over him as the footsteps retreated. But it was short-lived. A few hours later, the distant sound of barking grew louder. Bloodhounds.

Jared rushed outside, his heart sinking as he saw the search party returning, this time with dogs. The handlers barely paused, the hounds pulling eagerly on their leashes as they led the group straight to Jared's barn. The dogs circled beneath the loft, barking furiously.

"There's no one up there," Jared said quickly, stepping forward. "There's no ladder to get up, see?"

"Well, the dogs have picked up a scent and they led us here," the dog's handler said.

Chess's heart raced. He could hear the frantic barking directly below him, the sound vibrating through the wooden floor. The searchers were gathering, their suspicion growing.

Seeing the dogs, Isaac returned. "We need to get up there," Isaac said firmly.

Jared crossed his arms, his jaw tightening. "And how do you plan to do that without a ladder?"

Isaac exchanged glances with another man. They fetched a long board from a nearby pile, propping it against the loft's edge to climb up. Chess froze, every muscle tense as Isaac carefully balanced and ascended.

Isaac moved hay out of the way. Then asked for a stick. He poked the stick around. After a long, tense moment, Isaac sighed in frustration. "He's not up here," he called down.

Jared exhaled quietly, relief flooding through him. But he knew it was only a matter of time before Chess couldn't hide anymore.

CHAPTER 13

Florence and Carter arrived at Wilma's house, their faces weary and drawn. They had been part of the search team in the helicopter, scanning the vast stretches of land from above.

Florence shrugged off her jacket, her eyes shadowed with exhaustion. Carter followed, his expression grim. Wilma sat in her usual armchair, and Iris was perched on the edge of the couch, her face pale, her hands twisting nervously in her lap.

"No sign," Carter said, shaking his head. "We covered every possible route he could've taken from the air."

Florence added softly, "The bloodhounds lost the scent near Debbie's house. After that, nothing."

Wilma nodded slowly, absorbing the words, her gaze distant. Iris's eyes filled with unshed tears as she leaned forward, her voice a whisper. "But he has to be somewhere. He wouldn't just disappear."

"We checked every outbuilding and field in a five mile

radius," Carter added quietly. "Nothing turned up. It's like he vanished."

The silence that followed was heavy, punctuated only by the faint creak of the old house settling. Florence finally spoke, her voice gentler. "We're not giving up, Iris. We'll find him."

Iris nodded, though her shoulders trembled slightly. She wiped at her eyes, trying to summon strength she didn't feel.

"We think he's still close by," Florence murmured. "He couldn't have gone far on foot. Someone might be hiding him."

Wilma's gaze sharpened. "Hiding him? Why would anyone do that?"

Carter turned from the window, his jaw set. "Maybe to protect him. Maybe he's scared."

Iris's voice broke through the quiet. "Or maybe he's hurt."

No one responded immediately. The fear in her words hung in the air, too heavy to dismiss.

Wilma finally broke the silence. "We need to think about where he might go if he was frightened. Somewhere familiar, somewhere he feels safe."

Florence nodded. "We'll regroup at first light. We'll need to widen the search area and double back over the ones we've already checked."

Iris wrapped her arms around herself, staring at the flickering flame in the lantern. "He's annoying, but I just want him home," she whispered.

Wilma looked over at Iris. "We're going to bring him back. No matter what."

CHAPTER 14

The following day, Ada and Adaline stepped inside Wilma's house, and Wilma greeted them warmly, closing the door behind them.

"Any news on Chess yet?" Ada asked, wasting no time.

"No. People are out looking again today. They had the bloodhounds out yesterday and even a helicopter. Carter and Florence are going back out in the helicopter today."

"Where's Iris? I thought she'd be here," Adaline said.

Wilma gestured toward the window that overlooked the orchard. "She's been out there for some time. I'm not sure what she's up to."

Adaline's brow furrowed briefly before she nodded. "I'll find her," she said decisively, turning and heading out the door before anyone could object.

Ada watched her go, then turned her sharp gaze back to Wilma. "Now, tell me—what did Daniel want yesterday? I didn't want to ask too much in front of Adaline and Iris."

Wilma sighed, motioning Ada to the kitchen. "Come on in and have some tea. I'll tell you everything."

Ada followed her into the cozy kitchen, where Wilma set a kettle on the stove and began gathering the tea set. As she worked, she recounted Daniel's visit.

"He's developed feelings for Grace," Wilma said, her voice tinged with both concern and guilt. "Real feelings."

Ada's eyes widened, and she shook her head slowly. "This was never meant to happen. What will we do?"

Wilma poured the hot water into the teapot, her movements measured. "I'm not sure. He came to me for advice about their dates. It's clear he's taking this seriously."

Ada pursed her lips, tapping her fingers on the edge of the table. "Maybe we shouldn't let him in on the secret that we were only trying to make Matthew jealous."

Wilma set the teapot on the table and joined Ada, pouring the steaming liquid into their cups. "I agree. But meanwhile, does Matthew even care? Does he notice at all?"

Ada took a sip of her tea, shaking her head again. "Well, at supper the other night, he did seem like he wanted to walk Grace out, but Daniel beat him to it."

Wilma's lips pressed into a thin line. "Grace deserves someone who truly wants her, someone who will show it. If Daniel's the one, then maybe we've been looking at this all wrong."

Ada frowned, setting her cup down with a soft clink. "But what if Matthew does care? What if he's just slow to act? We could be steering this whole thing in the wrong direction. And Grace… well, she's sweet, but she's no fool. She'll catch on if we meddle too much."

Wilma leaned back in her chair, her gaze drifting to the window. "Maybe we should stop meddling altogether," she said softly. "Let them figure it out on their own."

Ada gave her a sharp look. "Matchmaking is not meddling. You don't mean that. You've been orchestrating this from the start. You don't let go of plans so easily."

Wilma chuckled lightly, conceding the point. "True. But it's becoming more complicated than I expected. Feelings are getting involved—real ones. If we keep going, we might hurt them all more than we help them."

Ada considered this, her fingers wrapping around her teacup. "You might be right. But if Daniel keeps coming to you for advice, it won't look like meddling. It'll just be you being a good listener and gently steering him. Perhaps we can find another lady for Daniel."

Wilma sighed, her thoughts drifting to Grace. She hoped the girl's heart wouldn't be caught in the crossfire of their schemes. "I'll keep an eye on things," she said finally. "And I'll keep being a good listener. But I think we need to tread carefully from here on out."

"If that's what you think is best, Wilma."

"I do."

CHAPTER 15

Meanwhile, Iris followed Matthew through the orchard, her heart light as she listened to him talk about the upcoming harvest. Matthew carried a small notebook, jotting down notes as he checked the trees, his focus entirely on the work at hand.

"It's going to be a good harvest this year," he said, pausing to inspect a particularly full branch. "The rain we had last week helped a lot, and the trees have bounced back nicely. I think we'll be able to start picking next week."

Iris smiled, brushing her fingers along the rough bark of a nearby tree. "The harvest has always been my favorite time of year. There's something magical about everyone coming together to pick the apples and sort them. It's a lot of hard work, but it's the best kind of work."

Matthew nodded, his lips curving into a small smile. "It is. And it's rewarding to see the fruits of all that effort. Literally."

They both laughed, the sound carrying through the quiet

orchard. Iris felt a warmth in her chest that had nothing to do with the sunlight. She enjoyed these moments with Matthew, when it felt like the rest of the world melted away.

"What's your favorite variety of apple?" she asked, tilting her head curiously.

Matthew thought for a moment, tapping his pencil against the edge of his notebook. "I'd have to say Honeycrisp. They're sweet, but with just the right amount of tartness. And they're great for baking."

"Good choice," Iris agreed. "I'm partial to Fuji apples. They're so crisp and juicy, and perfect for eating fresh."

"Fuji's a solid pick," Matthew said, his eyes twinkling. "You can't go wrong with a good apple."

Before Iris could respond, a voice called out, startling her. "There you two are!"

Iris turned to see Adaline making her way through the rows of trees, her dress swishing around her knees. She felt her stomach sink slightly, though she quickly masked her disappointment with a polite smile.

"Adaline, what brings you out here?" Iris asked.

"I was looking for you," Adaline replied, her gaze flicking between Iris and Matthew. "I thought I'd join you two for a bit. It's too nice of a day to stay inside."

"Of course," Iris said, though she couldn't help but feel a twinge of irritation. She'd been enjoying her time alone with Matthew, and Adaline's sudden appearance felt like an intrusion.

"Wilma had an interesting visit from Daniel. I'm not sure what he wanted."

Matthew's head whipped around. "That's odd."

"He had that date today with Grace. Or maybe it was yesterday. Yes, yesterday."

Matthew swallowed hard. "They had a date?"

Adaline covered her mouth with her hand. "Oh sorry. I thought you knew."

"No. No one said anything to me, but why would they? It's none of my business."

Iris and Adaline exchanged a glance. They both knew that something had happened on their date and Daniel had been reporting back to Wilma.

"Has Chess turned up yet?" Adaline asked, glancing around as though he might suddenly appear.

Matthew shook his head. "No."

"I hope he's okay, but I have a feeling he's taking some time alone. I would too if I'd started a fire. I'd wait until tempers had cooled and people were starting to worry a little about me."

Matthew gave a laugh.

"Do we know anything more about the fire? How it started?" Adaline asked.

"Not much," Matthew said. "It sounds like it was an accident, but we still don't know all the details."

Iris stayed quiet, letting the conversation flow around her. She didn't want to let on how much the fire and its aftermath had been weighing on her mind.

"It's such a shame," Adaline said, sighing. "That old shop held so many memories. But I suppose things can always be rebuilt."

"That's true, and maybe there's a reason for it all. Who knows?" Matthew said.

Iris glanced at him, her heart fluttering at his optimism. He had a way of seeing the silver lining in everything, and she admired that about him. Still, she couldn't help but wish she could have continued their lighthearted conversation about apples instead of diving into heavier topics.

"So, Wilma said you were walking out here, Iris. Are you walking or talking?"

Iris was a little shocked at Adaline's bluntness. She sure took after her grandmother.

Matthew laughed and answered for her. "She's doing both. She walked to get here and now she's talking to keep me entertained while I work. I'm grateful for that. It's lonely work out here sometimes."

Iris didn't know how to take that. Was she mere entertainment to him? "I guess I'm doing both, like he said." She smiled back at Adaline as though her words about 'walking or talking' hadn't bothered her. "I'm ready to go back to the house if you'd like me to walk back with you."

Adaline shook her head. "I think I'll stay out here for a while with Matthew."

Iris was so shocked that her mouth fell open.

Matthew turned around to face both of them. "I'll come back to the house too. It's time I had a break."

Adaline smiled back at him. Iris noticed the way her gaze lingered on Matthew for a moment longer than necessary. Could Adaline like Matthew too?

As they walked toward the house together, Iris focused on the sound of their footsteps and the rustle of leaves, trying to push her irritation aside.

The three of them walked in relative silence for a while, the orchard's serene beauty serving as a backdrop. Iris cleared her throat, searching for a way to break the awkwardness. "Matthew, said the harvest might begin next week, Adaline."

"Oh good. I can't wait. Are you excited, Matthew?"

"I am. It's always a busy time, but it's rewarding. Seeing everyone come together to get the work done is one of my favorite parts of the year."

"Do you think we'll have as many helpers as last year?" Iris asked, hoping to keep the conversation flowing.

Matthew shrugged. "It's hard to say. Some of the younger ones have taken on jobs elsewhere, but the community always pulls through. We also have the seasonal workers. I'm sure we'll manage."

Adaline added, "I've heard the apple pies this year are going to be legendary. Everyone's been talking about the new recipe someone brought from Ohio."

Iris forced a smile, even as her irritation simmered beneath the surface. She had to admit, Adaline had a knack for making conversation, even if it was about some imaginary new recipe. It sounded ridiculous.

"You've been working hard today," Iris said to Matthew as they approached the house. "Do you ever get a day off?"

Matthew chuckled. "Not often, but I don't mind. It's satisfying work. Besides, I wouldn't know what to do with myself if I had too much free time."

Romeo the cat darted toward Matthew, his fluffy tail high in the air as he wove around Matthew's legs, purring loudly. Iris blinked in surprise. Romeo was notoriously selective, yet here he was, rubbing against Matthew as if they were old friends.

Adaline smirked. "Well, that's unexpected. Romeo really seems to like you."

Matthew crouched down and picked up Romeo.

Iris folded her arms. "He usually keeps his distance."

"Maybe he can tell I'm not so bad after all," Matthew teased.

Iris wasn't sure how to respond to that, so she said nothing, watching as Romeo purred even louder as they kept moving toward the house.

CHAPTER 16

Sunday morning dawned gray and heavy with clouds, promising rain. Matthew hitched the buggy and drove Wilma and Iris to the bishop's house early, the wheels cutting through the damp earth with a soft, rhythmic crunch.

Inside the bishop's house, benches had been arranged in neat rows, the wooden floors polished to a soft sheen. The room filled gradually with the quiet murmur of voices, the shuffling of feet, and the occasional cough. Men sat on one side, women on the other, as was customary.

When the meeting began, voices hushed, and the bishop stood to address the gathering. His voice was solemn. "I have an announcement. Wilma's grandson, Chess, is missing. We ask that everyone keep an eye out for him. If anyone has seen or heard anything, please come forward."

A ripple of murmurs passed through the crowd, but quickly faded as the meeting continued. Iris glanced at Wilma, her face tight with worry, but Wilma sat with her back straight, her expression composed.

After the meeting, the rain began in earnest, forcing everyone to stay inside for the meal. The bishop's house felt crowded, the warm air thick with the mingling scents of homemade bread, pickled vegetables, and fresh pies. People gathered in small clusters, balancing plates of food and exchanging quiet conversations.

Tabitha, Wilma's granddaughter, weaved through the crowd with determined steps and tugged at Wilma's sleeve. "Mammi, I can find Chess. The dogs lost the scent around Jared's house—I mean Debbie and Gabe's house. So he must've been there at some point. Maybe he's still there. What do you think about that?"

Before Wilma could respond, Cherish appeared, her expression a mix of apology and exasperation. "Tabitha, what did I tell you about blabbing all the time?" She gently guided her daughter away, glancing back with an apologetic smile. "Sorry, *Mamm*. She talks way too much sometimes. She has six different ideas about where Chess might be, but the men have searched every one of those places."

"Thanks for your ideas, Tabitha," Wilma said.

Tabitha frowned and stared at her mother as she was being led away. "No, Mamm, I have only one idea where he is. I told you this already."

Wilma exchanged a glance with Ada, who raised her eyebrows meaningfully. Then they both noticed Daniel and Grace standing near the corner, speaking in hushed tones, their body language shy and awkward.

Ada couldn't resist. She leaned in and poked Wilma, nodding toward Matthew, who stood alone, his expression dark and brooding. "Look at him. Doesn't look too pleased, does he?"

Iris was next to Wilma and she overheard. "I'll go talk to him."

Wilma took the opportunity of no one around to hear them. "We still have to find out about what happened in Ohio. Let's not forget that. My memory is terrible, so you'll have to remind me."

"Yes, because no one will be interested in Grace because of what happened in Ohio. Isn't that what Daniel said, Wilma?"

"That's right on the very day we were trying to match him up, but what could it be? And he doesn't seem too bothered by it from the way he's looking at her."

A FEW MINUTES BEFORE, Daniel stood near the corner of the crowded room, his fingers lightly grazing the rim of his empty cup, the faint hum of conversations filling the space around him. Grace approached, her steps tentative but determined, her gaze flickering briefly to his before settling on the floor.

"Daniel," she greeted softly, her voice barely rising above the murmur of the room.

He glanced up, his face lighting with a smile that softened the sharp lines around his eyes. "Grace. I was hoping I'd see you here."

She tucked a loose strand of hair behind her ear, a shy smile tugging at the corner of her lips. "It's a small gathering today because of the rain. It's a bit hard to miss each other."

Daniel chuckled, the sound low and warm. "True. But still, I was hoping you'd come up to talk."

They stood in silence for a beat, the unspoken weight of their first date lingering between them.

"I enjoyed our date," Daniel said finally, his thumb tracing idle circles on the cup. "It was nice—peaceful. And your company was even better."

Grace's cheeks flushed a soft pink. "I enjoyed it too. It's been a long time since I felt that comfortable with someone."

He nodded, his gaze meeting hers fully now. "I was wondering... would you like to do that again? Maybe tomorrow afternoon, if the rain lets up? Or we could do something else if you'd prefer."

Grace's smile grew, genuine and warm. "I'd like that. The weather doesn't bother me much, but if it's raining, we could visit the bakery. I hear they've got fresh peach pies this week."

Daniel's eyes lit with amusement. "Now you're speaking my language. I can't say no to peach pie. It's a deal."

They shared a laugh, the tension easing slightly.

"How's your family?" Daniel asked.

Grace's smile faltered for a moment, but she quickly recovered. "Which one. I've got two families now."

"Oh yeah."

"They're both fine. When I'm here, I miss my other family. When I'm there, I miss my family here."

Daniel nodded thoughtfully. "Family can be complicated. But they're also our greatest strength, even when we don't see it right away."

Grace studied him, the sincerity in his words settling over her like a warm blanket. "You're right. It's just hard sometimes splitting myself in two."

"I know," he replied quietly. "If you ever need someone to talk to, I'm around."

Her heart gave a small, unexpected flutter. "Thank you, Daniel. That means a lot."

The rain outside intensified, a steady drumming against the windows. Daniel glanced toward the door, then back at Grace. "Looks like we'll be here a bit longer."

"I don't mind," she said softly, her eyes meeting his again.

They stood there, the world around them fading into the background. Daniel cleared his throat, shifting slightly. "You know, I was nervous to talk to you today. I didn't want to seem too eager."

Grace's laughter was light, easing the last of the tension. "I was nervous too. Funny how we make things more complicated in our heads."

"Maybe that's part of the charm," he mused. "The anticipation."

She nodded. "Maybe. But I'm glad we talked."

"Me too."

Silence settled again, but it was comfortable now. Daniel took a small step closer. "Grace, I don't want to rush anything, but I'd like to get to know you better. Not just walks and pie, though those are great. I mean really know you."

Her heart skipped, the sincerity in his voice grounding her. "I'd like that too, but that takes time."

He smiled, a slow, genuine curve of his lips. "I have loads of time."

"Good."

"Then it's settled. Wednesday, rain or shine."

"Wednesday," she echoed, her smile lingering long after he walked away.

~

Iris approached Matthew and then stood beside him. "You better put a smile on your face because people are watching you."

Matthew's jaw tightened. "Yeah, well, it's hard to put a smile on my face unless I genuinely got something to smile about. I'm not bothered by what people say. I've given up being bothered by it years ago."

Iris followed his gaze, which drifted to Grace, then flickered away quickly.

Iris wondered silently what Grace had that she didn't. Maybe Matthew still saw her as a child, not as a woman. She didn't know what to do to change that, and the thought gnawed at her heart.

"Anyway, I'm still thinking where your brother could've gone. Did your folks ask his friends?"

Iris nodded. "Dad went to all their homes and they didn't know anything. Dad was confident none of them were lying or trying to cover for him."

"He'll come back when he's ready. I'm sure of it," Matthew said.

"I know. I'm not worried. I'm only upset that he's caused so many people so much trouble."

Outside, the rain poured harder, drumming against the windows and the roof. It was soon time to leave, and the families gathered their things, bundling children into shawls and hats, preparing for the wet journey home.

CHAPTER 17

The chatter of the market swirled around Iris as she walked alongside Wilma, her arm linked with her grandmother's. The aroma of freshly baked bread and roasted peanuts filled the air, mingling with the laughter and voices of the bustling crowd. It was one of those lively market days, full of energy and familiar faces. But Iris's attention was snagged when she spotted Jared at a nearby stall.

"There's Jared," she said, nodding toward him. He stood at a vendor's cart, his back partially turned to them, but it was unmistakingly him.

"Let's go say hello," Wilma suggested.

As they approached, Jared shifted slightly, and Iris caught a glimpse of what he was trying to conceal—a small container of butternut, chocolate chip, and banana-flavored ice cream. Iris blinked. That was Chess's favorite flavor. Her heart skipped a beat, suspicion prickling at her.

Jared turned to face them, his expression startled but quickly smoothing into something neutral. "Oh, hi there," he said, his voice a little too casual.

"Hello, Jared," Wilma said warmly. "What brings you to the market today?"

"Oh, just picking up a few things," he replied, shifting the ice cream behind his back as subtly as he could. But Iris didn't miss it.

"What's that?" Iris asked, her voice sharp enough to make Jared flinch.

"Nothing important," Jared said quickly, glancing at the ground. "Just a little treat for myself."

Iris raised an eyebrow but didn't press further. She exchanged a look with Wilma, who seemed to catch on to her unease. After Jared said his goodbyes and hurried off, Iris turned to her grandmother.

"Did you see that?" Iris asked, her voice low. "That was Chess's favorite ice cream. Why would Jared be buying that?"

Wilma's brow furrowed, her expression thoughtful. "You think he knows something about Chess?"

"I don't know," Iris admitted. "But it seems suspicious. What if he's hiding him?"

Wilma nodded slowly. "Let's not confront him just yet. If Jared knows where Chess is, we'll find out soon enough. That ice cream won't last forever in this heat."

They decided to follow him, keeping a safe distance as they trailed his buggy back to his house. Jared didn't seem to notice them, his focus on the road ahead. When he pulled into his property and stopped near the barn, Iris's heart raced.

"He's going to the barn," she whispered, watching as Jared

grabbed the container of ice cream and headed straight for the building.

Wilma pulled their buggy to a stop a little way down the road. "Let's go," she said.

They crept toward the barn, staying low and quiet. The door creaked slightly as Jared opened it and slipped inside. Iris and Wilma exchanged a glance before hurrying closer, their footsteps muffled by the soft dirt.

Iris reached the door first and peered through the crack, her breath catching at the sight before her.

Chess was sitting cross-legged on a hay bale, looking pale and guilty. He held a spoon in his hand, the open container of ice cream between him and Jared. But what surprised her most was seeing Tabitha there too, perched on another hay bale, already working on her own portion of the ice cream.

Iris pushed the door open with more force than she intended, stepping inside. "What's going on here?" Her voice echoed.

"Oh thank goodness!" Tabitha exclaimed, jumping up from her hay bale and nearly dropping her spoon. "I was wondering how long it would take you to figure it out and show up here. I've been trying to convince these two they need to come clean."

Chess froze, his spoon halfway to his mouth. Jared stood abruptly. "Iris," Jared started, but Tabitha cut him off.

"Let me explain," she said, stepping forward. "I knew Chess would come here. I mean, where else would he go? Jared is kind and he wouldn't give him up. Jared is a man who is an individual, he'd make up his own mind, if you know what I mean. I told Mamm the other morning, I said, 'Mamm, I think Chess is at Jared's place,' but did she listen? No, she just kept on with her baking like I hadn't said a word."

"Tabitha," Wilma began, but Tabitha was on a roll.

"So I took Mamm's horse and buggy and came straight here. Found them both looking guilty as anything. Been here almost two hours now, trying to talk some sense into them. Chess hasn't said much, but I told him—"

"Tabitha," Iris interrupted firmly. "Let Chess speak."

"Well, I'm just saying what needs to be said," Tabitha insisted, crossing her arms. "Someone has to, and nobody else seems willing to—"

"Please," Wilma said gently but firmly. "We need to hear from Chess."

Chess set the spoon down, his hands trembling. "I'm sorry," he said quietly. "I didn't know where else to go."

"He really didn't," Tabitha interjected. "You should have seen him when I got here. All shaking and scared. I told him right away he needed to—"

"Tabitha!" Iris and Wilma said in unison.

Wilma stepped further into the barn. "Chess, what happened?" she asked gently.

Chess looked down at his hands, his shoulders slumping. "It was an accident," he said, his voice cracking. "I was in the shop, and I lit a candle. I didn't think… I didn't mean for it to happen."

"The fire?" Wilma asked.

"I knew it was an accident!" Tabitha burst out. "I told everyone it had to be. Chess would never—"

Jared reached over and put a hand on Tabitha's arm. "Let him tell it," he said quietly.

A tear trickled down Chess's face. "The candle must've got knocked over somehow. I panicked and ran. I didn't know what else to do."

"Which is exactly why he needed someone to talk to," Tabitha added, though more softly this time. "I found him here this morning, barely eaten anything since he arrived. That's why I went to the market myself to get his favorite ice cream, but Jared had the same idea. We've been trying to convince him to—"

"You went to the market too?" Iris asked, momentarily distracted. "We only saw Jared there."

"Oh, I went earlier," Tabitha explained. "But the ice cream cart wasn't open yet. I told Jared when he got here that Chess needed ice cream, and he went straight back to town. I would have gone again myself, but Mamm's probably already noticed her buggy's missing, and I didn't want to push my luck, though honestly, she never listens to me anyway, so maybe she hasn't even—"

"Can we focus?" Iris asked, feeling a headache coming on. She turned back to Chess. "You've been here the whole time?" Iris felt a lump rise in her throat as she watched him. For all his mistakes, Chess looked utterly broken, a boy weighed down by guilt and fear.

"And you came here?" Wilma asked.

Chess nodded again. "Jared said I could stay. He's been helping me."

"We've all been helping him," Tabitha corrected. "Well, at least since this morning when I got here. Someone had to make sure he was thinking straight, and these two were just sitting here being all quiet and guilty and—"

Wilma turned to Jared. "Why didn't you tell us? Carter and Florence have spent loads of money on searches and dogs, helicopters. And everyone's time has been wasted searching."

"I tried to get him to," Tabitha interjected. "I told him this morning that keeping secrets never—"

"Tabitha," Wilma said firmly, "I think it's time for you to head home. I'll speak with your mother tomorrow."

Tabitha's eyes widened. "Am I in trouble? I mean, I was only trying to help, and someone had to do something, and—"

"That will be between you and your mother. You need to get home right now or there'll soon be a search party out for you!"

"But I want to—"

"Tabitha. Please."

Tabitha's shoulders slumped, but she nodded. "Fine. But I still think I did the right thing," she added, heading for the barn door. She paused at the entrance. "You'll let me know what happens, won't you, Jared?"

"Goodbye, Tabitha," Wilma said pointedly.

"Thanks for everything," Jared called after her.

After Tabitha finally left, Jared ran a hand through his hair, looking ashamed. "I didn't want to betray him," he admitted. "He was terrified, and I thought he needed time to figure things out. I was going to tell you eventually. He was never going to stay beyond a few days, but I thought he'd know when he was ready."

Wilma sighed deeply, and turned to Chess. "You have to take responsibility for what happened. Running away won't fix anything."

"I know," Chess whispered. "I'll make it right. I'll do whatever it takes."

Iris crossed her arms, her emotions a whirlwind of anger, pity, and something she couldn't quite name. "You should have come to us," she said quietly. "We could have helped you."

"I was scared. I thought everyone would hate me."

"We don't hate you," Wilma said firmly. "But you need to face the consequences of your actions. That's the only way to move forward."

Chess nodded. "Okay,"

"Let's get you home," Wilma said.

The ride back to Chess's house was quiet except for the sound of the buggy's wheels crunching over the gravel road. Chess sat between Wilma and Iris, his hands clenched tightly in his lap. He wasn't sure what to expect when they got home. Would his parents be angry? Disappointed? He wouldn't blame them if they were furious—he'd let everyone down.

As they pulled into the yard, Florence and Carter raced outside. Florence's face lit up as soon as she saw Chess step down from the buggy.

"Chess!" she cried, rushing forward to throw her arms around him. "I'm so happy you're safe."

Chess froze for a moment, caught off guard by her reaction. He'd expected yelling, maybe even a lecture, but her embrace was warm and full of relief.

"We've been worried sick," his dad said, stepping up behind Florence and placing a hand on Chess's shoulder. "Where have you been?"

Chess swallowed hard, the lump in his throat making it difficult to speak. "I... I was running away," he admitted, his voice barely above a whisper. "I didn't mean to... I didn't know where else to go."

Florence pulled back, cupping his face in her hands. "What happened, Chess? Why did you feel like you had to run?"

He looked down, ashamed to meet her gaze. "I think the fire was my fault," he said. "I was hiding out in Grandma's shop, and I lit a candle. It must've fallen over when I wasn't paying attention. I… I'm so sorry."

Florence's eyes filled with tears, but she didn't look angry. Instead, she pulled him into another hug. "You're safe, and that's what matters right now. We'll figure everything else out."

Carter nodded in agreement. "We'll fix it together. You don't have to handle this on your own, son."

Chess blinked, stunned by their kindness. He'd been so sure they'd be furious, but here they were, offering him nothing but support. It made the guilt in his chest feel even heavier.

Wilma cleared her throat gently. "We should be going," she said. "I'm glad he's home, but there are some people we need to tell about this good news. He can tell you where he's been." She turned to Iris, a soft smile on her face. "Do you want to spend the night here with your family?"

Iris hesitated for a moment before shaking her head. "No, I'll come with you. Let's tell Ada and Adaline that we've found Chess."

Wilma's smile widened. "I think that's a wonderful idea."

Chess watched them climb back into the buggy, his heart swelling with gratitude. "Thank you," he said quietly. "For everything."

Wilma nodded. "Bye, Chess. Don't worry so much."

"Thanks, Grandma. I'm sorry for everything."

As the buggy disappeared down the road, Chess turned back

to his parents. For the first time in what felt like forever, he felt a flicker of hope.

CHAPTER 18

Finding Chess had been a relief, but the tension of him running away still lingered. Iris glanced at her grandmother, who seemed lost in her own thoughts.

"I'm glad we found him," Iris said softly. "But do you think he'll be okay? I'm talking mentally. He's got a lot of problems. Those bad friends of his don't help."

Wilma sighed, her gaze fixed on the road ahead. "He's a good boy at heart. With the right guidance, he'll find his way."

Iris nodded, her fingers twisting in her lap. She couldn't help but think about how much Chess had been carrying on his own. It made her wonder what she would do in his shoes—whether she'd have the strength to face everyone after making such a mistake.

"Ada and Adaline will be happy to hear the good news."

When they arrived at Ada's house, Ada opened the door before they knocked.

Wilma wasted no time. "We found Chess. He's back home now, safe and sound."

Ada's expression softened with relief. "Thank goodness. That boy had everyone worried sick."

Adaline appeared behind her grandmother. "You found him? Where was he?"

"Hiding out at Jared's," Iris said, a hint of amusement in her tone. "Eating ice cream, of all things."

Adaline giggled. "Oh, well if you're going to hide, you might as well do it with ice cream.'

"And you'll never guess who else was there," Wilma added, settling into her favorite chair. "Tabitha."

Ada's eyebrows shot up. "Tabitha? How did she—"

"Borrowed her mother's buggy without asking," Iris explained. "She'd apparently figured out where Chess was hiding and took matters into her own hands."

"That sounds like Tabitha, from what I know of her," Adaline said, trying to suppress a smile.

"Oh, you should have seen her," Wilma continued, shaking her head. "We could barely get a word in edgewise. Every time Chess tried to explain himself, there was Tabitha, telling us how she knew all along, how she'd tried to tell everyone, how she'd gone to get ice cream earlier but the stand wasn't open yet..."

Ada burst out laughing. "That's why her brothers call her Blabitha! Yes, that's a bit unkind," she added, catching Wilma's look, "but I feel their frustration. That girl could talk the ears off a corn stalk."

"I had to send her home," Wilma said. "She was so worried about being in trouble with her mother, but she still managed to ask three more questions on her way out the door."

"Did anyone know he was there?"

"Jah. Where do you think he got the ice cream from? Iris figured it out. We came across Jared at the markets and Iris noticed he had a bucket of Chess's favorite ice cream in his hands. We followed him home and we found Chess."

"Jared knew all along?" Ada asked.

"It seems so."

"Hmm, it wouldn't occur to Jared that so many people would be worried about him."

"I think that Jared was more thinking about Chess's feelings. He's very kind. I'm going to a craft show with him," Adaline said.

Iris was pleased to hear it. "Well Tabitha sure gave Jared an earful about that. She told us she'd spent two hours trying to convince them both to come clean."

"Well, between Tabitha's talking and Chess's conscience, something had to give," Wilma mused. "I'll have to stop by Cherish's tomorrow, see how she took the news about her daughter's little adventure."

Ada laughed, "Though knowing Tabitha, she's probably already told her mother the whole story. Twice."

"And added a few extra details each time," Adaline added with a giggle.

"You know," Iris said thoughtfully, "for all her chatter, Tabitha did do the right thing. She knew where Chess was and made sure he wasn't alone. Even if her way of helping was... well, very Tabitha."

"That's true," Ada agreed. "Though I suspect Cherish might have preferred a less dramatic way of finding out where her buggy disappeared to."

The four of them settled into the living room, the tension from earlier slowly unraveling. The relief of finding Chess had finally sunk in, and with it came a bit of amusement at the way everything had played out.

"I still can't believe he was just sitting there eating ice cream," Adaline said, shaking her head.

Ada huffed a laugh. "And I still can't believe Tabitha managed to keep it to herself for as long as she did."

"She didn't," Wilma said dryly. "She just didn't have an audience yet."

That sent another round of laughter through the room.

CHAPTER 19

When Iris and Wilma got home, Iris lingered on the porch for a moment, her gaze drifting toward the orchard. That's when she saw Matthew walking back toward the house, his steady stride cutting through the rows of trees bathed in the golden hues of the setting sun.

Without hesitation, she stepped off the porch and hurried to meet him. "Matthew!" she called out, her voice carrying across the open space.

He paused, turning to see her approaching. His face lit up with a warm smile. "Hey, Iris. What's going on?"

She stopped a few steps away, catching her breath. "They found Chess!" she said, her words tumbling out quickly. "He's back."

Matthew's brows lifted in surprise. "Really? That's good news. Where's he been?"

"Hiding out at Jared's place," she explained. "He didn't

mean to start the fire. He said he was running away with Romeo."

Matthew chuckled softly. "Running away with a cat? That sounds like something Chess would do."

"I know," Iris said with a small laugh. "He said it was an accident, the fire. A candle must've tipped over in the shop."

Matthew nodded thoughtfully. "At least he's safe. That's what matters most."

They began walking back toward the house together, their steps falling into an easy rhythm while Iris told him how they found Chess.

"That was clever."

"Thanks. Funny that I found him because of the ice cream."

"What did Jared say about hiding him?"

"Nothing much. Maybe he'll get into trouble off his mom."

"Possibly."

"You're late getting home tonight. Is it because the harvest is coming soon?"

He nodded. "Yeah, it's our busiest time of year. It's busy, but rewarding. There's something about seeing everyone come together to get the job done—it's special."

"I love it. I've always loved harvest and that first day and the big cookout and all."

"It's a tradition."

"Grace could be there," Iris pointed out, watching his reaction closely. "How will that make you feel?"

He shrugged, his gaze fixed on the path ahead. "Sometimes people just want different things. We had our moments, but in the end, it wasn't meant to be."

Iris chewed on her bottom lip, debating whether to say

more. Finally, she ventured, "People have been talking, you know. They think you seem... weird about Grace dating Daniel."

Matthew stopped walking, turning to face her with a furrowed brow. "They're dating?"

Iris blinked, caught off guard by his question. "Didn't you know?"

He shook his head, his expression a mix of surprise and confusion. "I thought they went on one date. Dating is a huge leap."

"I'm not sure what's going on," Iris admitted. "It's just what people are saying."

Matthew rubbed the back of his neck, a faint frown tugging at his lips. "Neither do I. But it's not really my business anymore, is it?"

They resumed walking, the silence between them stretching for a few moments. Iris stole a glance at him, her curiosity still gnawing at her. "Does it bother you?" she asked carefully. "The thought of her with someone else?"

He exhaled slowly, his gaze thoughtful. "I'd be lying if I said it didn't sting a little at first. But honestly? I want her to be happy. If Daniel makes her happy, then that's a good thing."

Iris studied him, searching for any hint of lingering feelings.

"Do you think they're a good match?" Matthew asked suddenly, catching her off guard.

Iris hesitated, caught off guard by the question. "I think... I think she deserves someone who'll put in the effort. Someone who'll make her feel special."

Matthew smiled faintly. "That's fair."

As they reached the porch, Iris turned to him, her curiosity still nagging at her. "Matthew, do you ever think about what could've been? With Grace, I mean."

He paused, his hand resting on the railing. "Sometimes, but I think things worked out the way they were supposed to. God has a way of putting you where you're meant to be. Can we forget her? I really don't want to keep talking about her."

Iris nodded, his words settling over her like a blanket. She wasn't sure what she'd expected him to say, but his honesty made her heart ache in a way she didn't fully understand.

As they stepped onto the porch, the sound of laughter drifted from inside the house. Iris glanced at Matthew, his profile illuminated by the warm light spilling through the windows. In that moment, she realized how much she valued his presence, his steadying influence in her life.

"Thank you for walking with me," she said softly.

He turned to her, his smile gentle. "Anytime, Iris."

They stepped inside together, and found Wilma laughing at the cat as she teased Romeo with a piece of string. Wilma abruptly stopped when they walked in.

CHAPTER 20

The morning sun was warming Wilma's kitchen when she heard the familiar sound of buggy wheels approaching. She glanced out the window to see Cherish's buggy pulling up, with Tabitha practically bouncing in her seat beside her mother. Even from this distance, Wilma could see Cherish's taut expression – the look of a mother who'd had a very long morning.

Before Cherish could fully stop the buggy, Tabitha was already jumping down, her words tumbling out before she even reached the porch. "Mammi! Tell Mamm everything that happened about how I found Chess. And how I knew exactly where he'd be. I told her all about it, but she says she needs to hear your side of the story, which doesn't make sense because my side is perfectly clear and—"

"Tabitha," Cherish interrupted, climbing down from the buggy more carefully. "Let's at least get inside before you start."

Wilma opened the door, welcoming them both with a warm

smile. The kitchen smelled of fresh-baked bread and coffee, and Tabitha immediately zeroed in on the plate of cookies on the counter.

"Oh! Did you make these this morning? They look just like the ones my friend Emma's mamm makes, except hers are usually a bit darker on the bottom because she always gets distracted by her baby, but these look perfect, and—"

"Tabitha," Cherish said again, this time with a slight edge to her voice. She turned to Wilma. "I'm sorry if she got in the way of what was going on yesterday. And about the buggy..." She shot her daughter a meaningful look.

"I took it without asking," Tabitha admitted, though she didn't sound particularly repentant. "But honestly, Mamm, it's not like it was hard to drive. It's just common sense, and I have loads of that. Just ask anyone! I'm like way older than my age in years. I'm practically like a twenty-one-year-old."

Wilma couldn't help but laugh at that declaration, while Cherish looked increasingly frazzled. "Oh?" Cherish raised an eyebrow. "If you're twenty-one, maybe you should do the work of a man out in the dairy."

Tabitha's nose wrinkled. "No, the cows are a bit smelly. I think I'll work in the orchard when I get older. Or I might grow flowers. I love flowers. Did you know I've been reading about different types of roses? There are so many kinds! And some of them smell amazing, while others don't smell at all, which seems like a waste of a rose if you ask me, because what's the point of a rose if it doesn't—"

"Tabitha," Wilma interjected gently, "why don't you go out to the garden with Iris? She's working on the new flower bed, and

I'm sure she'd love to hear about what you've learned about roses."

Tabitha's face lit up. "Oh! Yes! I can tell her about the climbing roses I read about. They'd look perfect on that trellis by your back gate. And maybe we could plant some lavender too. I read that lavender and roses go well together, and—"

"Go on now," Wilma encouraged, and Tabitha practically bounced out the door, her voice trailing behind her as she spotted Iris in the garden.

Cherish sank into a kitchen chair with a heavy sigh. "That child," she said, but there was fondness mixed with the exasperation in her voice. "Sometimes I think she was born talking and just never saw a reason to stop."

Wilma poured them both coffee and set out the cookies. "She means well," she said, sitting down across from Cherish. "And she did help yesterday, in her own way. Chess needed someone to care, even if that someone talked his ear off in the process."

Cherish wrapped her hands around the warm coffee cup. "I know. And I'm pleased for her wanting to help. I just wish she'd gone about it differently. Taking the buggy without asking..." She shook her head. "What if something had happened? I had no idea she was gone."

"But nothing did," Wilma pointed out gently. "And now she knows better. Sometimes the lesson is in the learning."

They could hear Tabitha's voice drifting in from the garden, explaining something about soil pH to Iris with great enthusiasm. Cherish smiled despite herself. "I suppose. Though I did give her quite a talking-to about the buggy. Not that I could get many words in. Anyway, how is Chess doing? Really?"

"As well as can be expected. He's carrying a heavy burden of guilt, but that's not necessarily a bad thing. It means he understands the gravity of what happened."

Cherish nodded slowly, then hesitated before asking, "What are you thinking about the shop? It's plain to see there's not much of it left. Just the foundations really."

Wilma's face grew thoughtful. She'd been turning this question over in her mind since yesterday. "That's actually something I wanted to discuss with you. It'll have to be demolished, of course. The fire damage is too extensive. I could build the shop again but it's getting no use. Or should I build something else?"

"What's the foundation like?" Cherish asked, her practical nature coming to the fore. "Is it still solid?"

"Seems to be. The fire didn't damage it much, but it's old. Dat built it himself, so you girls could sell apples and other goods there. But you didn't use it much before you went out on the roadside stalls."

"I know but there wasn't much traffic going past the house all those years ago. The fact that Dat built it makes it harder to think about removing it."

"Jah," Wilma admitted. "But I have to think practically. Do I just get rid of the foundations altogether and have nothing there or build something else, maybe something different?"

Outside, they could hear Tabitha exclaiming over something in the garden, followed by Iris's gentler voice offering suggestions. Cherish glanced toward the window. "What are the options if you keep the foundation?"

"Well, we could rebuild the shop, maybe make some improvements to the layout. The old one was a bit cramped in places. Or..." Wilma paused, considering. "We could do something entirely different with the space. I've been thinking about that too."

"Different how?"

"The community's growing. We could use more gathering spaces, maybe something that could serve multiple purposes. A place for the young people to learn crafts, or for meetings, or even just somewhere to sit and visit."

Cherish nodded thoughtfully. "That could be good. The youth need more places to gather that aren't someone's house or the schoolhouse." She paused, then added with a small smile, "Though maybe we should make sure it has good soundproofing if Tabitha's going to be there."

They both laughed at that, the tension of the serious discussion breaking for a moment. Through the window, they could see Tabitha gesturing animatedly while Iris nodded, seemingly absorbed in whatever detailed explanation of floriculture she was receiving.

"The foundation itself would need to be inspected properly," Wilma continued, returning to the practical matters at hand. "I don't want to make any decisions until we know exactly what we're working with."

"That's wise," Cherish agreed. "And what about Chess in all this? Should he be involved in the rebuilding, whatever form it takes?"

Wilma considered this carefully. "I think he needs to be and I'm sure Florence and Carter will see that he is."

They discussed the specifics for a while longer – costs, timing, who might be able to help with the work. The morning sun climbed higher, warming the kitchen further, while outside

Tabitha's voice continued to babble like a brook after a heavy rain.

Finally, Cherish glanced at the clock. "We should be going. I've got washing to do, and if I don't start soon, it'll be dark before I finish." She stood, then hesitated. "About Tabitha... I know she can be a handful, but her heart's in the right place."

"That it is," Wilma agreed warmly. "And sometimes, Cherish, those who talk the most just have more love to share. They just need to learn how to measure it out a bit better."

Cherish smiled, grateful for the understanding. "I do tell her that all the time. Tabitha!" she called through the open window. "It's time to go home now."

"But I haven't finished telling Iris about the heritage roses," Tabitha's voice floated back. "Did you know some of them have been growing for hundreds of years? There's this one kind that—"

"Tabitha. Now."

They could hear a dramatic sigh, followed by rapid-fire farewell words to Iris. Moments later, Tabitha burst back into the kitchen, still talking. "Mammi, your garden is amazing! But you really need more varieties. I was just telling Iris about this beautiful climbing rose that would look perfect on the north side of the house, and there's this spot by the gate that's just begging for a butterfly garden. I know exactly what we should plant there. First, you'd need some—"

"Tabitha," Cherish interrupted firmly. "The washing. We have to go."

"Oh, right. But can I come back and help with the garden sometime? Please? I have so many ideas, and Iris said she'd love to learn more about companion planting, which I've been reading about, and it's fascinating how certain flowers grow better together, just like people, really, when you think about it, and—"

"We'll see," Cherish said, already moving toward the door. "Thank you for the coffee, Mamm. And the talk."

"Of course. You should stop by more, but I know you're busy."

"I'll come instead if Mamm let's me take the buggy," Tabitha offered.

Cherish frowned at Tabitha. "When you're older."

As Tabitha and Cherish headed back to their buggy, Tabitha's voice carried on the morning breeze, explaining something about soil amendments to her mother.

Wilma watched them go, a small smile tugging at her lips. She'd once told Cherish that she hoped she'd have a daughter just like herself one day—so she could understand exactly how exasperating she could be. She never really thought it would happen.

CHAPTER 21

Jared's fingers drummed against the buggy's wooden seat as he pulled up to Ada's house. He'd spent twenty minutes this morning reorganizing his tool shed instead of getting ready, and now he was running a few minutes late. Still, he couldn't help but feel pleased with how the shed looked – everything had its proper place now, at least until he needed something and pulled it all apart again.

Adaline was already waiting on the porch, her dark blue dress making her eyes seem brighter somehow. She hurried down the steps, calling a goodbye to her grandmother who stood in the doorway.

"Sorry I'm a bit late," Jared said as he helped her up into the buggy. "I got caught up with... something." He didn't mention the tool shed. It seemed silly now.

"Oh, that's fine," Adaline smiled, settling beside him. "I was just reorganizing my grandmother's spice shelf anyway. Did you know she had three containers of cloves? And they weren't even next to each other!"

Jared laughed, recognizing the familiar need to put things in order. The buggy started forward, and he found himself relaxing into Adaline's company. She was easy to be around – she understood when his attention wandered or when he needed to stop and adjust something that wasn't quite right.

The craft show was being held in the community center, and already Jared could see the colorful displays through the windows as they approached. Inside, tables lined the walls and created neat rows through the center of the room. Quilts hung from the rafters, their patterns casting dancing shadows on the floor.

"Oh, look at these!" Adaline exclaimed, moving toward a display of carved wooden animals. She picked up a small deer, then set it down and adjusted its position slightly. Picked it up again. Moved it a fraction to the left. "There. Now it looks right."

Jared understood completely. He'd been fighting the urge to straighten every crooked picture frame they passed. "The craftsmanship is good," he said, examining the deer. "But the grain could have been better aligned here." He pointed to a spot on the deer's neck.

"I see that now. You have a good eye for things."

Jared beamed at the compliment.

They moved through the show together, stopping frequently to examine items that caught their attention. Jared found himself watching Adaline as much as the crafts – the way she'd touch things gently, adjust their positions, step back to look, then adjust them again. She did it unconsciously, just as he did.

She was like the female version of himself and that was appealing.

"I don't see any wooden birdhouses," Adaline said, scanning the woodworking section. "You should really have some here. Your work is better than everything I'm seeing."

Jared shuffled his feet, suddenly aware of the empty space where his work could have been. "I was going to enter some, actually. Had three nearly finished. But then... I got an unexpected visitor and didn't get to finish painting or anything." He trailed off, thinking of Chess hiding in his barn.

Adaline giggled, a sound that made something warm flutter in Jared's chest. "I still can't believe you were hiding Chess all that time. What did Debbie say about that?"

"My mother doesn't say too much to me anymore. I'm an adult – I really do what I want." Jared adjusted the corner of a tablecloth that had been bothering him for the past five minutes. "She just said it probably wasn't a good idea, but I told her the kid needed some time alone to think through what he'd done."

"I know that's true," Adaline said, absently rearranging a display of corn husk dolls into perfect alignment. "But what about all the people worried about him? Did you stop to think about them?"

"Well, I reckon that's their problem. They didn't need to worry. They should've trusted that he could look after himself. He's old enough." Jared watched as Adaline stepped back to examine her work with the dolls, then moved one slightly to the right. "Sometimes people need space to figure things out don't you think?"

"I guess."

They continued through the show, stopping at a quilting display where Adaline spent several minutes making sure all the hanging quilts were exactly level with each other. Jared helped, finding comfort in the precise measurements and adjustments. It felt natural, working together like this.

"These candlesticks are crooked," Adaline murmured, reaching for a brass display. "And look, the prices aren't even lined up properly."

Jared helped her straighten the items, their hands occasionally brushing as they worked. Each touch sent a little jolt through him, making him wonder if she felt it too. Was this a date? He wanted it to be, but maybe she just saw him as a friend who understood her need to fix things, to make them right.

They spent nearly fifteen minutes reorganizing a table of preserves by color and jar size. The seller looked amused but didn't stop them – the display did look better afterward. Jared loved how Adaline didn't question the time spent on such tasks, how she dove in with the same enthusiasm he felt.

"Are you hungry?" he asked. "There's a food stand outside."

"Starving," Adaline admitted. "Though we should probably straighten those wreaths by the door before we go out. They're all hanging at different heights and it's making me twitchy."

Jared grinned. She was definitely his perfect match. "I've been trying not to stare at them for the past hour."

They fixed the wreaths, got their food, and found a quiet spot to eat. Adaline had a smudge of powdered sugar on her chin from her fasnacht, and Jared had to resist the urge to brush it away. Instead, he found himself talking about his birdhouses, describing the new designs he wanted to try.

"You should definitely enter them next time," Adaline said firmly. "Promise me you will? Unless you're hiding any more runaways in your barn."

"No more runaways," Jared laughed. "Though I have been thinking about building a proper workshop out there. The current setup isn't organized right. Everything's just a little bit off, you know?"

Adaline nodded enthusiastically. "Like when all the cups on a shelf are different heights and you can't line them up properly?"

"Exactly like that!"

The afternoon passed too quickly. They made one more circuit of the show, adjusting anything that wasn't quite right, talking about everything and nothing. Jared found himself noticing small details about Adaline – the way she tugged on her prayer kapp strings when she was concentrating, how her nose crinkled slightly when something was out of alignment, the sound of her laugh when he said something funny.

As they drove back to Ada's house, Jared couldn't stop wondering about what this had been. A date? A friendly outing? The buggy wheels clicked against the road in a rhythm that seemed to match his thoughts: Ask her, ask her, ask her.

"I had a wonderful time," Adaline said as they pulled up to the house. She paused before getting down, adjusting the hem of her dress so it lay perfectly straight. "We should do this again sometime. Maybe you could show me your birdhouses and where you work?"

Jared's heart leaped. "I'd like that," he said, trying to keep his voice steady. "Maybe next Sunday afternoon if you aren't doing anything?"

"Perfect." Adaline smiled, and this time Jared was sure he

wasn't imagining the slight blush in her cheeks. "And this time, try not to get distracted by any unexpected guests."

She hurried up the porch steps, turning to wave before disappearing inside.

Jared sat in the buggy for a moment longer, a grin spreading across his face. He reached down to adjust the edge of the buggy's cushion one last time before heading home, his mind already full of plans for next Sunday and hopes about what it might mean.

CHAPTER 22

Chess's house was still and quiet, but Florence lay awake, staring at the ceiling of her and Carter's bedroom. The events of the previous day played over and over in her mind. Chess was home, safe and sound, but the weight of what had happened—the fire, his running away, and his guilt—hung heavy in the air.

Beside her, Carter sighed deeply, shifting on the mattress. Florence turned to face him, her voice low. "You're still awake too?"

"How could I sleep?" Carter replied, his voice tinged with weariness. "We've got a lot to do tomorrow. First thing, we'll need to go to the police and explain what happened."

Florence nodded, her heart tightening. "Do you think they'll press charges?" she asked quietly.

Carter hesitated, then shook his head. "I don't know. I don't think so. It was an accident, but accidents can still have consequences. Whatever happens, Chess will have to face it. It's the only way he'll learn."

Florence sighed. "And after that, we'll go to Wilma's. She'll want to decide what to do with the shop."

"There's not much of it left," Carter said, his voice heavy. "It's a shame. That place held so many memories."

Florence reached out, placing a hand on his arm. "We'll help her rebuild, if that's what she wants. It's the least we can do."

Carter nodded, his gaze distant. "I just hope this is a turning point for Chess," he said after a moment. "He's been so lost lately. Trying to impress those older boys, getting into trouble… It's like he's looking for something, but he doesn't know what."

"He's a good boy at heart," Florence said softly. "He just needs guidance."

Carter sighed again, rubbing a hand over his face. "Sometimes I feel like I'm losing both of them," he admitted, his voice barely above a whisper.

Florence frowned. "Both of them? What do you mean?"

"Chess to those boys," Carter said, his tone grim. "And Iris to the Amish. It's not what I wanted for her. When you left the community all those years ago and we had children, I thought we were giving them a chance at a different kind of life. One with more freedom, more opportunities. But now…"

"You think she's slipping back into it," Florence finished for him.

Carter nodded. "She's so close to Wilma, and I know she loves her time on the orchard. But it's more than that. She's spending so much time with Matthew, and I see the way she looks at him. She's got feelings for him, even if she won't admit it. And he... he's Amish through and through. If they ever ended up together, she'd be drawn back into that world."

Florence was quiet for a moment, her thoughts swirling. "Is that so bad?" she asked gently.

Carter's jaw tightened. "I don't want her to lose herself," he said. "The Amish way is good and honest, but it's not for everyone. She's experienced life outside of it. If she doesn't experience this life, will she regret it? Will she miss the freedom she had?"

"Iris is strong," Florence said. "Whatever she decides, she'll make it work. And Matthew is just a passing crush. She'll get over him."

Carter let out a long breath, his shoulders sagging. "Maybe you're right," he said. "But it's hard to let go, you know? She'll always be my little girl."

Florence smiled, reaching out to take his hand. "She'll always be ours, no matter where life takes her."

They were silent for a while, the weight of the day's events settling over them like a heavy blanket. But as the minutes passed, Florence felt a flicker of hope. Chess was home, and Iris was finding her own path.

∼

THE RAIN TAPPED STEADILY against the window, a rhythmic, relentless sound that matched the heaviness in Chess's chest. He lay sprawled on his narrow bed, staring at the ceiling as shadows shifted with each flash of distant lightning. The faint scent of smoke still lingered on his clothes, a bitter reminder of the mess he'd made. He rolled over, burying his face in his pillow, but sleep wouldn't come. His mind replayed the events over and over like a broken record.

The flames had licked the walls of his grandmother's shop, devouring everything in their path. It was Wilma's heart, filled with memories, laughter, and the quiet creaks of years gone by. And he… he had reduced it to ash. He hadn't meant to. It was an accident. But accidents had consequences. That was the part he couldn't shake.

Chess sat up abruptly, running a hand through his unruly hair. His room felt like a cage, the walls closing in, filled with silent accusations. He wanted to punch something, to scream, to escape. But where would he go? His friends had all turned their backs the moment things got tough. Real friends wouldn't have dragged him into that mess in the first place.

His gaze drifted to the window. The rain had intensified, blurring the outline of the apple trees beyond. Their dark, twisted branches looked like clawed fingers reaching for something just out of reach. He pressed his forehead against the cool glass, his breath fogging a small circle. If only he were older. If only he could make his own decisions. He'd pack a bag, hitch a ride, and disappear. No more lectures, no more disappointments, no more screwing things up.

But he wasn't an adult. He was just Chess—the kid who couldn't do anything right.

His chest tightened as he thought about his parents. They were downstairs, whispering about what to do with him. Maybe they'd called the police already. Maybe they were filling out forms, deciding his fate.

Juvie.

He'd heard that word more than once on the drive home. The word felt like a brand, searing into his brain. He didn't want that. He wasn't a bad kid. He'd just made some stupid choices.

And then there was Iris. Perfect, sweet Iris, with her big eyes and her holier-than-thou attitude. Pretending she wanted to be Amish, like that made her better than him. She got to be the good kid, while he was the screw-up. She even had Romeo purring in her lap at Grandma's house, probably not missing him at all. It wasn't fair.

Chess flopped back onto the bed, staring at the ceiling again. His fists clenched at his sides. Why did everything have to be so complicated? Why couldn't he just be invisible for a while, fade into the background until people forgot how much he'd messed up?

He closed his eyes, but sleep remained elusive. Instead, memories crept in—of Wilma's smile as she baked pies in the shop, of Iris laughing under the apple trees, of his dad teaching him how to fix a bike chain. They weren't just random flashes; they were weights, each one pressing down harder than the last.

Chess sat up again, unable to stay still. He paced the small room, his bare feet cold against the wooden floor. The rain outside seemed to mock him, its relentless patter a reminder that the world kept turning, even when his had fallen apart.

He paused by the window, looking out at the drenched orchard. The trees stood tall, unbothered by the storm. Strong. Resilient. Why couldn't he be like that? Why did he always crumble when things got hard?

His reflection in the glass stared back, a distorted version of himself with tired eyes and a frown etched deep. He hated that face. Hated the guilt, the regret, the fear. But it was all his. No one else to blame.

Sliding down to sit against the wall, Chess pulled his knees to his chest. Maybe facing the consequences was the only way to fix this.

The rain continued, a steady drumbeat against the window, as Chess sat in the dark, waiting for morning.

CHAPTER 23

At breakfast time Iris, seated across from Matthew, found her gaze flitting toward him more often than she liked to admit. Romeo, her ever-curious cat, prowled around the room, stalking invisible prey beneath the table.

"This smells wonderful, Wilma," Matthew said, as he spooned steaming oatmeal into his bowl. "Nothing beats one of your breakfasts to start the day."

"I'm glad you think so. It's simple, but it'll keep you going until lunch," Wilma replied with a smile.

Iris silently agreed, focusing on her food and hoping her cheeks didn't betray her thoughts. Matthew's presence always seemed to have a way of unsettling her composure, though she doubted he noticed.

As they ate, the conversation drifted to the day ahead. Matthew shared his plans for the orchard, the morning dew still clinging to the trees, and how they'd need to check on the trees after last night's storm.

"You've done good work. The orchard's been in my family for generations, and it's comforting to know someone's working there and being passionate about it."

Matthew smiled, a hint of pride in his expression. "I've been thinking about doing something else as well."

Wilma raised an eyebrow. "Oh? What's on your mind?"

Matthew set his spoon down. "I've been considering joining the volunteer firefighters."

The room fell quiet for a moment. Iris's heart skipped a beat, the words taking her by surprise. She glanced at Wilma, who'd leaned back slightly in her chair, clearly pondering the idea.

"That's a noble decision. Many of the Amish men in our community are involved with the fire department. It's a way to give back, to serve. I think it's a wonderful idea."

Iris, however, felt a jolt of anxiety ripple through her chest. She stared at her bowl, her appetite fading. "But it's dangerous," she blurted, the words escaping before she could stop them. "You could get hurt. Or worse."

Matthew's gaze shifted to her, and she felt the weight of his attention. "There's always risk, but it's worth it if I can help people. Fires can destroy lives, and if I can do something to stop that, why wouldn't I?"

"What about the smoke?" Iris pressed, her voice a little sharper than she intended. "Breathing it in, being in those conditions… It's not just risky; it's…" She trailed off, struggling to articulate the words.

Wilma gave her a curious look, but Iris avoided meeting her gaze. Romeo leapt onto her lap, purring as he kneaded her dress with his paws. She stroked his fur absently, trying to calm herself.

"I appreciate your concern, Iris. I've thought this through. The department offers training, and they take precautions. It's not a decision I'm making lightly."

Iris nodded, but her mind whirled with unspoken arguments. She wanted to tell him to reconsider, to think about what he'd be leaving behind if something went wrong. But she knew she couldn't. It wasn't her place to say those things, not without revealing more than she intended.

"You'd be good at it. You've got the strength and the calm demeanor for that kind of work. People would look up to you."

Matthew's expression softened. "Thank you, Wilma. That means a lot."

Iris bit her lip, her thoughts a tangled mess. She knew she should say something supportive, but every word that came to mind felt loaded with the emotions she was trying to hide. Instead, she focused on Romeo, who had settled into her lap and was batting at the edge of the tablecloth.

"What do you think, Iris?" Matthew's question caught her off guard.

Her head snapped up, and she met his gaze. For a moment, her mind went blank. Then she forced a small smile. "I think it's... admirable," she said carefully. "But just... be careful, okay?"

Matthew nodded, his expression unreadable. "I will."

The conversation shifted to lighter topics, but Iris found it hard to focus. Her mind kept circling back to the thought of Matthew rushing into burning buildings, risking his life. She hated the idea, not just because it was dangerous, but because it underscored how little control she had over her feelings for him.

When breakfast ended, Iris helped clear the table, her movements automatic. Matthew excused himself to head out to the orchard, leaving her alone with Wilma.

"You were awfully vocal about Matthew's plans," Wilma said, her tone light but curious. "You've never struck me as the worrying type."

Iris's cheeks flushed. "I just… I don't like the thought of anyone getting hurt, that's all."

Wilma didn't press, and she didn't seem to notice anything out of the ordinary.

Later, as Iris sat in her room with Romeo curled up beside her, she replayed the morning in her mind. Had she been too obvious? Had her worry betrayed her feelings? She groaned softly, burying her face in her hands.

"I've got to get a grip," she muttered. "He probably didn't even notice."

But deep down, she wasn't so sure. Romeo stretched, his tail flicking lazily, as if to say he wasn't concerned about her problems. Iris envied his simplicity. If only her own emotions were so easy to manage.

CHAPTER 24

Wilma wiped her hands on her apron as the sound of Ada and Adaline's buggy approached the house. She stepped onto the porch, smiling as Ada climbed down cautiously.

"Look at you!" Wilma called out warmly. "It's nice to see you without that bandage."

Ada flexed her arm slightly with a grin. "Feels good to have it off, but I still have to be careful."

"Mammi insisted on packing this herself," Adaline explained, carrying a basket of fresh produce. "She wouldn't let me help."

"Of course she didn't," Wilma teased, stepping forward to take the basket. "What do we have here?"

"Vegetables some need ripening, but I picked them now so the birds wouldn't get them," Adaline said.

As they moved into the kitchen, a streak of orange shot between their feet, followed by Iris's frustrated voice from inside. "Romeo! No! Get back here!"

The cat darted through the open door and across the yard. Iris appeared moments later, her face flushed. "He's been impossible all morning," she told Wilma.

They watched as Romeo raced down the driveway, just as Carter and Florence's car was pulling up. The cat darted past their wheels, heading straight for Chess, who was walking up the path.

Chess caught Romeo mid-stride, lifting him easily. The cat immediately settled in his arms. Iris stopped short, her expression hardening.

"I can take him back to the house," Chess offered. "It's easy to see he loves me the most."

"He's fine where he is, with me," Iris replied, crossing her arms.

"I think we can leave the cat here with Iris if Wilma doesn't mind," Florence suggested as she stepped out of the car.

"I don't mind at all," Wilma assured them. "I find Romeo quite entertaining."

"See this as part of your punishment, Chess," Carter added, looking pointedly at his son.

Chess's jaw tightened, but he nodded, carefully transferring Romeo back to Iris. Their hands didn't touch during the exchange, both being careful to avoid contact. "Why didn't you wake me up?" Chess asked his parents.

"We thought you needed the sleep," Carter replied.

Adaline narrowed her eyes. "You both arrived at the same time though."

"We had business in town earlier," Florence explained, and Chess must've been coming here to apologize, right Chess?"

"Yes." He looked over at Wilma. "I'm sorry, Grandma."

"It was an accident. It's fine. You've already apologized."

"We came to talk about the shop," Florence announced, turning to Wilma. "We think it's time to decide what's next and we want to help."

Wilma sighed, looking toward the burned building. "I've been giving it a lot of thought and I realize something. It's not just my decision. The orchard belongs to all of us—the whole family."

"We've spoken to everyone, Wilma," Florence responded. "They're happy to leave it up to you. This is where you live."

Romeo squirmed in Iris's arms, stretching toward Chess. "You can hold him while you're here," Iris said handing him back to Chess.

"I've been torn," Wilma admitted, glancing at the charred remains of the shop visible in the distance. "I've been considering several options. We could rebuild it as it was, or perhaps make it into something new entirely. I've thought about a community gathering space, or maybe expanding the apple butter kitchen..."

"I have an idea," Chess announced, stepping closer to the group while maintaining his distance from Iris.

"Well, go on. Tell us," Ada encouraged.

"Why not make it into a tiny house?" Chess suggested. "Matthew's friends could pitch in. I'll do a lot of work too. I can even do most of it."

"That's good thinking, Chess," Florence said warmly.

"What do you think about that idea?" Carter asked Wilma, raising an eyebrow.

"It's an interesting thought," Wilma responded carefully. "I'll need to consider it along with the other possibilities. A guest house could be useful, but I'm also thinking about what would best serve the orchard's needs."

"But how would it be paid for?" Florence asked, looking at Chess.

"I'll pay!" Chess declared. "I'll get a job."

"Chess, rebuilding takes time—and money," Carter reminded him, placing a hand on his son's shoulder.

"I don't care," Chess insisted. "I'll work hard. I promise." He kept his eyes fixed on his father, deliberately not looking at Iris.

"We'll see," Wilma said thoughtfully. "Let's take it one step at a time. Right now, we have a harvest to prepare for. We have to focus on that for now. There's no rush to decide about the shop."

"Chess will be here helping, won't you?" Florence prompted, looking at her son.

"Of course. I'm always here for the harvest." Chess replied.

"And don't bring any of your friends," Iris told him.

"They wouldn't be interested anyway."

"So what will you do about the shop, Wilma?" Adaline asked.

"I'm still weighing all the options," Wilma answered. "The tiny house is an interesting idea, but I want to think through everything carefully before making any decisions. The foundation is still good, which opens up a lot of possibilities. I've been thinking about maybe a larger workspace for the apple canning, the apple drying, or perhaps a store to sell our products year-round. That is, if someone makes the commitment to run it. We'll need to consider what will be most practical in the long run."

Florence glanced at her watch. "Well, we should be going.

Chess has chores waiting at home." She touched Chess's arm gently. "Come on, son."

Chess nodded, his eyes lingering briefly on Romeo, who was still sprawled in his sunny spot on the porch. Carter gathered the tools they'd brought to inspect the foundation, and the three of them headed to their car.

When Florence and Carter left with Chess, the others went back to Wilma's house. Adaline went upstairs to see Iris's sewing projects while Wilma and Ada stayed in the kitchen gossiping.

CHAPTER 25

The kitchen was warm and fragrant with the smell of fresh-baked cookies and brewing tea. Wilma could hear Adaline and Iris still giggling upstairs as she set out her best teacups for herself and Ada. Romeo had followed the girls up, no doubt hoping for attention now that Chess was gone.

"So," Ada said, settling into her favorite kitchen chair, "I have some news that might interest you." She picked up a cookie, examining it with a smile. "Adaline went on a date with Jared yesterday."

Wilma nearly dropped the teapot. "What? A date?"

"Mhmm," Ada confirmed, clearly enjoying Wilma's reaction. "To the craft show."

"But..." Wilma set the teapot down carefully. "She mentioned they were going to the craft show the other day. Isn't Adaline so much older than Jared?"

Ada laughed, shaking her head. "No, they're the same age. I

don't know why you keep thinking Adaline is so old all the time, Wilma."

Wilma bit her lip, settling into her chair. "She just seems so mature, and Jared..." She shrugged, wrapping her hands around her warm teacup. "He just seems like the naughty little boy that used to live in this house."

Ada chuckled, dunking her cookie in her tea. "He's come a long way. I used to worry about him and his naughtiness, but he's grown up into a fine young man. One of my favorite people, ever."

Another burst of laughter drifted down from upstairs, followed by Romeo's curious meow.

"So," Wilma leaned forward eagerly, "did they call it a date? Was it a real date? Tell me everything – where did they go, what did they do, what did she say when she came back?"

"Well," Ada began, reaching for another cookie, "she came home absolutely glowing. They spent the whole afternoon at the craft show, and apparently, they share some... interesting habits."

"What do you mean?"

"According to Adaline, they spent nearly twenty minutes reorganizing a preserve display until all the jars were perfectly aligned." Ada's eyes twinkled. "She said Jared understood exactly why the different-sized jars being out of order was so bothersome."

"Oh!" Wilma's expression softened with understanding. "That does sound like both of them."

"And," Ada continued, lowering her voice conspiratorially despite being alone in the kitchen, "he asked her to come see his birdhouses next Sunday."

"A second date already?" Wilma smiled, remembering her own courting days. "And what did she say?"

"She said yes, of course. Though she's trying not to seem too excited about it." Ada sipped her tea thoughtfully. "You should have seen her trying to pick out her dress for the craft show. Changed three times, and then tried to pretend it didn't matter what she wore."

The sound of footsteps overhead turned into more giggling, and both women smiled.

"Speaking of courtships," Ada said, "have you heard about Grace and Daniel?"

Wilma nodded. "Only that they went on a date and I think a second one is planned."

"Oh dear. How does Matthew feel about Grace dating someone else?" Ada asked carefully.

Wilma shrugged, pouring them both more tea. "He wouldn't tell me how he feels. It makes me want to keep out of things now. I don't like matchmaking because it can get messy."

"Or it could end in marriage," Ada pointed out with a smile.

"That's true enough," Wilma conceded. "But sometimes I think we meddle too much. Look at how things worked out with Matthew and Grace – all that pushing and pulling, and in the end, they weren't meant for each other at all."

"But Daniel and Grace..." Ada prompted.

"They found each other despite our efforts." Wilma smiled. "Sometimes the best matches are the ones we don't arrange."

Ada nodded thoughtfully. "Like Jared and Adaline?"

"Exactly." Wilma paused as more laughter echoed from above. "Though I have to admit, I never saw that one coming. Jared always seemed so..."

"Scattered?" Ada suggested. "Restless?"

"Yes, but Adaline seems to understand him. And he's settled down so much in the past year. His business is doing well, he's responsible..."

"A far cry from the boy who used to put frogs in your flower pots," Ada remembered with a laugh.

"Oh, don't remind me!" Wilma groaned. "Though I have to admit, those birdhouses he makes are beautiful. Such detailed work. He's turned something that people wouldn't think about much into something that a lot of people now want."

"Adaline mentioned he was supposed to enter some in the craft show but got distracted with... well, you know." Ada's expression grew more serious. "With Chess."

Wilma nodded, understanding the unspoken complexity. "Speaking of distractions, how do you think Daniel's family feels about him courting Grace?"

"Oh, they're thrilled," Ada replied, clearly glad to move to a lighter topic. "His mother told me that she's never seen Daniel so happy."

More giggles drifted down from upstairs.

"Remember when we were that age?" Wilma asked softly. "Everything seemed so important, so exciting."

"Still is, for them," Ada said, reaching for another cookie. "Though I have to say, watching Adaline with Jared... it reminds me of watching you and Josiah when you were courting. The way she lights up when she talks about him."

Wilma smiled at the memory. "We barely courted. We got married so quickly. We both knew it was right. There was no point having a long courtship."

"I know. Now about the shop..." Ada's voice trailed off. "Do you think Chess's idea about the tiny house might work?"

"I don't know," Wilma admitted. "There are so many things to consider. But right now, I'm more interested in hearing more about this date. Did Adaline say anything else about what they talked about?"

Ada's eyes sparkled as she launched into more details about Jared and Adaline's day together, while upstairs, the girls continued to chat and laugh.

CHAPTER 26

Grace stood in front of the small mirror, adjusting her kapp for the third time, her heart thumping a nervous rhythm. The twins, Anna and Olivia, dashed around the room like excited puppies, their braids swinging and eyes sparkling with curiosity.

"Do you think she'll get married this time?" Anna asked in a loud whisper.

"Maybe! She's had two dates now! That's practically an engagement," Olivia giggled, clutching her sister's arm.

Grace sighed, trying to smooth the front of her dark blue dress, wishing she could smooth the fluttering nerves inside her just as easily. The twins' excitement only heightened her anxiety. She wasn't sure why Daniel had asked for another date, but she wasn't about to question it too much.

Christina appeared in the doorway, hands on her hips, her expression part amusement, part exasperation. "Alright, you two , out of here. Give Grace some peace."

"But we want to see her get ready!" Anna protested, her bottom lip jutting out in an exaggerated pout.

"Out," Christina said firmly, pointing towards the door.

With dramatic sighs, the twins shuffled out, whispering to each other, clearly plotting how to spy on Grace later.

Christina turned back to Grace, her eyes softening. "Don't worry about them. You'll be fine. Just be yourself."

Grace let out a shaky breath, her fingers fiddling with the edge of her apron. "Being myself hasn't got me anywhere. Do you really think that's a good idea?"

Christina laughed, crossing the room to push some loose strands of Grace's hair back into her prayer kapp. "Of course, you should be yourself. That's who he asked out, isn't it? Not someone you're pretending to be."

Before Grace could reply, a soft knock echoed through the house. Her heart skipped a beat.

"That's him," Christina whispered with a wink.

Grace moved to the door, her palms damp with nerves. She opened it to find Daniel standing there, his straw hat in his hands, dark hair slightly damp from the drizzle. His buggy was parked behind him, the horse shifting its weight patiently. Daniel's smile was warm, easing some of the tension coiled in Grace's chest.

"Hello, Grace," he said softly.

"Hello, Daniel." She stepped outside, pulling the door closed behind her. The cool rain-scented air wrapped around them.

He offered his hand to help her into the buggy, his fingers warm against hers. She settled into the seat, surprised to see a neatly packed basket tucked at their feet.

"I had planned a picnic," Daniel said, glancing at the gray clouds with a sheepish grin. "But the weather had other ideas."

Grace smiled. "Maybe the rain will stop."

They rode in comfortable silence, the rhythmic clip-clop of the horse's hooves blending with the soft patter of rain on the buggy's canopy. Daniel navigated the familiar roads with ease, steering them towards the nearby park where a waterfall tumbled gracefully over rocks, even more vibrant against the rain-soaked landscape.

The rain had lightened to a mist by the time they arrived. Daniel guided the buggy to a sheltered spot under a cluster of tall trees. The ground was too wet for a traditional picnic, so he spread a thick blanket across the back of the buggy, creating a cozy nook. Grace helped arrange the food: simple sandwiches, fresh fruit, and a jar of homemade lemonade.

They sat side by side, their shoulders occasionally brushing, sending sparks of awareness through Grace. The conversation flowed more easily this time, filled with laughter and shared stories. Daniel spoke of his work with the horses, his eyes lighting up with passion. Grace found herself drawn to the warmth in his voice, the kindness behind his words.

As they finished their meal, the rain finally ceased, leaving the world fresh and glistening. Daniel stood and offered his hand once more.

"Shall we take a walk? The waterfall looks beautiful after the rain."

Grace nodded, slipping her hand into his. They followed a narrow path along the edge of the waterfall, the roaring water a melodic backdrop to their quiet conversation. The ground was slick from the rain, the rocks mossy and uneven.

Grace took a cautious step, her foot slipping on a patch of wet stone. A gasp escaped her lips as she lost her balance, but Daniel reacted swiftly. His arms wrapped around her waist, pulling her against him, steady and secure.

For a heartbeat, they stood frozen, the only sound the rush of the waterfall and the thud of Grace's racing heart. She looked up, her breath catching as their eyes met. There was something different in his gaze, something deeper than friendship, something that made her knees weak.

His hands remained firm on her waist, his warmth seeping through the layers of fabric. Grace's heart hammered against her ribs, but she didn't pull away. Neither did he.

"Are you alright?" Daniel's voice was soft, barely louder than the water's roar.

Grace nodded, her words tangled somewhere between her heart and her lips. "Yes. Thanks to you."

They stood there a moment longer, the world narrowing to just the two of them. Finally, Daniel released her gently, his touch lingering like the warmth of the sun after a storm.

They continued their walk, but something had shifted, an unspoken connection woven between them. When they returned to the buggy, the silence was comfortable, filled with things left unsaid but understood.

As Daniel opened the door, their hands managed to touch. Grace felt a blush creep up her cheeks, but she didn't look away.

"Thank you for today," she said softly.

Daniel smiled, his eyes crinkling at the corners. "Thank you for coming."

The ride home was quieter, but the silence was filled with

warmth. When Daniel finally stopped in front of Grace's house, he raced around to open the door.

"Goodnight, Grace," he said softly.

"Goodnight, Daniel."

As she watched him drive away, Grace felt something she hadn't in a long time—hope.

Grace stepped into the cozy, dimly lit kitchen, her face flushed with excitement and the cool evening air. She set her purse on the table and kicked off her shoes, unable to contain the smile tugging at the corners of her mouth.

Christina looked up from her knitting, her keen eyes immediately noticing the lightness in her daughter's step. "Well, you're home early," she said, setting the knitting aside. "How did it go?"

Grace's heart swelled, and before she could think twice, the words tumbled out. "Mamm, I want to marry him. He's not distant like Matthew was. Matthew seemed like he wanted to be close and then he'd pull back. Daniel's nothing like that."

Christina's eyebrows shot up. She loved it when her daughter called her Mamm rather than by her name. It seemed that Grace hadn't even noticed she'd said it. She stood, walking over to Grace, her hands resting gently on her daughter's shoulders. "Does he feel the same way?" she asked softly, searching Grace's eyes for answers.

"I think so. We got along really well. Today was different—we're getting used to each other. There was this comfort, like we'd known each other longer than we have. I've got a good feeling about this, Mamm."

Christina pulled Grace into a warm embrace, her heart filled with hope and love for her daughter. "Me too," she whispered, holding her close. "I really do." Christina pulled back slightly, her hands still resting on Grace's arms. "Tell me everything. What did he say? What did you do?"

Grace's eyes sparkled. "It felt so natural. He listened, really listened, and when I spoke, he looked at me like what I had to say mattered. There was no awkwardness, no trying too hard. Just... ease."

Christina smiled, her heart swelling with joy. "That sounds wonderful, Grace."

"It was. And when we got here, there was this pause, you know? Like neither of us wanted to say goodbye. I could see it in his eyes—he feels it too."

Christina squeezed her hands gently. "Sometimes, when you know, you just know. And it sounds like your heart knows."

Grace let out a soft sigh, leaning her head against her mother's shoulder. "I think it does. I really think it does."

CHAPTER 27

Wilma woke with a heavy heart. She'd hardly slept, her mind tangled with thoughts of Grace and Ohio. Ada and she had totally forgotten to look into what Daniel had told them. He'd practically said it would be hard for Grace to find a husband after what happened in Ohio.

After tending to her morning chores, Wilma found Iris setting out a fresh batch of biscuits to cool. The aroma of warm bread mingled with the faint scent of lilacs drifting through the open window. Wilma wiped her hands on her apron and approached her granddaughter.

"Iris, I need you to stay here today," Wilma said.

Iris glanced up, her blue eyes narrowing slightly. "Why? Where are you going?"

"Ada and I are visiting Christina by ourselves," Wilma replied, reaching for a jar of preserves. "We've got some matters to discuss."

Iris's face tightened with frustration. "Why can't I come? I'm not a child, Wilma. I can help."

Wilma sighed, setting the jar down with a soft thud. "It's not about help. This is something Ada and I need to handle. You'll stay with Adaline. She could use the company."

Iris crossed her arms, her lips pressing into a thin line. "Why can't I come?"

Wilma's eyes flashed with a brief spark of irritation. "You'll stay with Adaline. That's final."

Iris huffed. "Seems like you don't trust me with anything important."

Wilma softened slightly, stepping closer. "It's not about trust. Sometimes grown folks have to handle things their own way. You'll understand one day."

Iris didn't respond, her silence thick with resentment.

Wilma arrived at Ada's house and Iris stayed there with Adaline.

Together, Ada and Wilma headed to Christina's.

"Iris wasn't happy about staying behind," Wilma admitted.

Ada chuckled softly. "She's at that age where everything feels like an injustice. Let her stew; it builds character."

Wilma managed a smile, though she was worried about hurting Iris's feelings.

When they arrived at Christina's house, the sight of the tidy yard and the twins playing with baby lambs brought a brief sense of peace. Christina greeted them with surprise but welcomed them inside without hesitation.

Inside, the familiar comfort of Christina's home wrapped around them. The scent of freshly baked bread mingled with lemon-scented polish. They sat around the wooden table, sipping cool lemonade and nibbling on slices of bread slathered with homemade jam.

Small talk flowed easily at first—discussions of gardens, upcoming gatherings, and the stubbornness of livestock. But beneath the surface, Wilma's thoughts churned, circling back to Grace and Ohio.

After what felt like an eternity, Ada cleared her throat, her voice gentle yet firm. "Christina, we came here with a purpose. We need to talk about Grace."

Christina's smile faded, replaced by a look of concern. "Grace? What about her?"

Wilma leaned in, her voice low. "We need to know what happened in Ohio. Did something… happen to her or did she do something?"

Ada added, "Something that might affect her future?"

CHAPTER 28

Christina blinked, confusion flickering across her face. "Ohio? I don't think Grace has ever been to Ohio."

Wilma and Ada exchanged puzzled glances.

"But, I'll find out. Grace deserves happiness, a family. If something's standing in her way, I want to know."

Wilma nodded slowly.

Then Christina hesitated, her gaze narrowing slightly. "Is this about the fire at your place, Wilma?"

Wilma's spine stiffened. "No," she replied quickly, waving the question away. "Nothing to do with that."

Christina studied her for a moment, clearly unconvinced but choosing not to press further. After a beat of silence, Christina added quietly, "You should know… Grace seems to be falling for Daniel."

"We had heard that," Wilma said with a nod.

"Yes. It's a bit of a surprise and hard to get used to seeing that she's been dating Matthew for so long."

As they left Christina's house, Wilma said to Ada, "What do we do now?"

Ada sighed, her gaze distant. "We let Grace follow her heart, but at the same time we keep an eye on Daniel. It seems he knows about what happened in Ohio and it's not holding him back from dating Grace."

"Very true, Ada, very true."

∽

WHEN GRACE and Mark returned home from the saddlery store, Christina was waiting with the twins, Anna and Olivia, who had been looking forward to Grace coming home. The faint creak of the screen door closing behind them echoed through the house.

"Grace!" the twins squealed in unison, jumping up from their coloring books spread across the kitchen floor. They rushed toward their older sister and Grace giggled as they wrapped their arms around her in a tight hug.

"The new shipment arrived late," Mark said, hanging his hat on the wooden peg by the door. "But we managed to get everything sorted before sundown. Grace was a great help."

Grace smiled at Mark while the twins tugged at her hands. "It wasn't like work at all. I really enjoy working there."

"I'll wash up before supper," he said.

"You girls go wash up too."

"Yeah, later," Anna said.

"No, now. I want to talk with Grace for a moment."

"But we want to stay with Grace!" Olivia protested.

"Go on now," Christina said firmly. "You'll have plenty of time with her at supper."

The twins reluctantly followed their father, casting longing glances at Grace as they left.

"Let's go into the kitchen," Christina said.

"Have I done anything wrong?" Grace asked as she poured herself a glass of cool lemonade.

Christina sat at the table, her fingers tracing idle patterns on the tablecloth. "Sit with me for a moment, Grace."

Grace raised an eyebrow but complied, settling into the chair opposite her mother.

Christina's eyes studied her daughter carefully. "I had visitors today. Ada and Wilma stopped by."

Grace set her glass down. "Oh? What did they want?"

Christina hesitated, her fingers pausing mid-pattern. "They seemed... concerned. About you."

Grace tilted her head slightly. "Concerned about me? Why?"

Christina's gaze didn't waver. "Apparently, they're worried about what happened in Ohio."

For a moment, silence hung heavy between them. Grace's expression remained unreadable, her fingers gently tapping the side of her glass. "What happened in Ohio?"

Christina leaned in slightly, her voice gentle but firm. "Well, apparently, you should know. It seems like you did something terrible in Ohio. It's okay, Grace. You can tell me. I'm your mother."

Grace pointed to herself, her brow furrowing. "Me? So, I'm supposed to have done something terrible in Ohio?"

Christina nodded slightly, her eyes searching her daughter's face for any hint of truth or denial. "I think so."

Grace's confusion turned into disbelief as she leaned back in her chair. "Maybe whoever has said this has the wrong person. I've never even been to Ohio."

The simple, matter-of-fact statement hung in the air, shifting the tension into something almost absurd. Christina blinked, her mouth opening slightly as if to respond but no words came immediately.

Grace didn't know whether to be annoyed or amused. "Seriously? They think I did something terrible in a place I've never been?"

Christina's lips pressed into a thin line, her mind racing to reconcile the absurdity of the situation. "Maybe there's some misunderstanding. Or perhaps they've confused you with someone else as you said."

Grace leaned forward, her elbows resting on the table. "Or maybe they just wanted to stir up trouble. As if they don't have enough of that in their lives already. Wilma's shop has burned down and Ada has Adaline visiting. Why do they waste time and energy like this?"

"I think they're trying to help." Christina sighed, rubbing her temples gently. "I just wanted to hear it from you, Grace. To be sure."

Grace's expression softened slightly. "I appreciate that, but there's nothing to tell. I haven't done anything in Ohio because I've never set foot there."

Christina nodded slowly, the tension in her shoulders easing slightly. "I believe you. It's just... they seemed so certain."

Grace reached across the table, placing her hand gently over her mother's. "Then maybe it's time to stop worrying about what they think."

Christina managed a small smile, squeezing Grace's hand gently. "You're right. I'm sorry I even brought it up."

"Next time they come with some wild story, just send them my way. I'd love to hear what I've supposedly done."

Christina chuckled softly. "I was worried and now I can breathe easy."

"I just hope that Daniel doesn't hear any of these rumors." Grace bit her lip thinking of the implications.

From down the hall came the sound of splashing and gleeful giggles, followed by Mark's gentle admonishment to the twins about leaving water everywhere. The familiar domestic sounds helped ease the tension of the moment.

"I'll visit Wilma tomorrow and find out what's going on," Grace said.

Christina shook her head. "I don't know if that's such a good idea."

"I think that's the only thing I can do."

CHAPTER 29

The following morning, Grace woke with a restless energy that refused to be ignored. The absurdity of the rumors gnawed at her like an itch she couldn't reach. As soon as she finished her work with Mark, she wasted no time borrowing the horse and buggy.

"I just need to clear my head," she told Mark when he raised an eyebrow about where she was going.

He nodded, wiping sweat from his brow. "Take your time."

The rhythmic clatter of hooves against the dirt road did little to soothe her growing frustration. By the time she reached Wilma's house, the tension in her chest felt like a tightly wound spring. She guided the buggy to a stop, climbed down with brisk efficiency, and marched up the front steps without hesitation.

Wilma answered the door, surprise flickering across her face before settling into her usual guarded expression. "Grace? I wasn't expecting you."

Grace didn't waste time on pleasantries. "I need to talk to you."

Wilma stepped aside, motioning her in. The house smelled faintly of fresh bread and lavender, but Grace was too agitated to appreciate it. She followed Wilma into the modest sitting room, her hands clenched at her sides.

"Why are you talking about Ohio?" Grace demanded, her voice sharp with frustration.

Wilma's brow furrowed. "What do you mean?"

"I mean someone's spreading rumors about me—saying I did something terrible in Ohio. But I've never even been there. So why are you telling people otherwise?"

Wilma's lips pressed into a thin line, her gaze dropping briefly before she spoke. "It's not like that. Ada and I were just concerned. Someone mentioned something... something that might make it hard for you to find a husband. That's what they said."

Grace stared, disbelief etched into every line of her face. "What? That's ridiculous! What did they say happened?"

Wilma shook her head slowly, her expression tinged with discomfort. "I don't know. That's all they said."

Grace took a step closer, her frustration boiling over. "Well, who said it? Who is 'they?' Is it one person or more than one person?"

Wilma's mouth tightened. "I don't know."

"You expect me to believe that? You're spreading around vague rumors without even knowing who started them?"

Wilma's face flushed slightly, but she remained silent.

Grace exhaled sharply, shaking her head. "Unbelievable."

Without another word, she turned on her heel and stormed

out, her steps echoing on the wooden porch. She was just about to climb into the buggy when a familiar voice called out.

"Grace, wait!"

She turned to see Matthew striding toward her, his expression filled with urgency. He reached her side just as she set one foot on the buggy's step.

"Did you come to see me?" he asked breathlessly.

Grace glared at him, her patience worn thin. "Is it you who's spreading rumors about me?"

Matthew froze, his face a mix of shock and hurt. "No. I've never said anything bad about you. Ever."

Grace's jaw tightened. "Well, someone is. They're saying I did something terrible in Ohio. But I've never even been there."

Matthew's brow furrowed deeply. "Would you like me to find out what's going on?"

Grace scoffed, climbing into the buggy with swift determination. "Just leave me alone. I want nothing more to do with you."

She snapped the reins, her horse responding immediately. The buggy jolted forward, the wheels crunching over gravel as she sped down the driveway, leaving Matthew standing alone.

~

IRIS HAD BEEN TENDING to the barn when she noticed Grace's buggy pulling up to Wilma's house. Curiosity got the better of her, and she lingered near the open barn door, pretending to check on a harness while keeping an eye on the scene unfolding outside. She watched as Grace stormed toward the porch with determined strides, her posture stiff with frustration.

Moments later, she saw Matthew approach Grace just as she was about to climb into her buggy. Their interaction was brief but intense, filled with sharp gestures and heated expressions. Iris couldn't hear every word, but the tension was undeniable. When Grace finally drove off, leaving Matthew standing there, staring after her, Iris felt a pang of something she didn't want to admit—jealousy.

She wiped her hands on her apron and strode out of the barn, her steps quick and deliberate. She approached Matthew, who was still standing like a statue, his gaze fixed on the disappearing buggy.

"You're still in love with her, aren't you?" Iris blurted out, folding her arms across her chest.

Matthew startled slightly, turning to face her. "No, not at all," he replied quickly, though his tone lacked conviction. "But I still like her as a—"

Iris raised an eyebrow, cutting him off. "Then why are you staring after her like that?"

Matthew sighed, running a hand through his hair in frustration. "Because she accused me of spreading rumors about her."

Iris's expression softened slightly, though the jealousy still simmered beneath the surface. "Did you?"

His eyes flashed with indignation. "Of course not! I would never do that. I'm not that kind of man."

Iris studied him for a moment, searching for any hint of dishonesty. But all she saw was genuine frustration and hurt pride. She took a step closer, her voice dropping slightly. "Then why does she think you are spreading rumors?"

Matthew shrugged helplessly. "I don't know. Maybe because

we've had our... history. Maybe she thinks I'd want to get back at her or something. But that's not who I am."

Iris felt a mixture of relief and lingering irritation. "Well, you sure looked like you cared a whole lot more—more than just friends."

Matthew narrowed his eyes slightly, sensing the edge in her voice. "Why do you care so much?"

Iris opened her mouth to respond, then closed it again, realizing she didn't have an answer she wanted to admit. Instead, she looked away, focusing on the dusty road where Grace had disappeared.

"I just don't like seeing people get hurt, that's all," she muttered.

Matthew let out a dry chuckle. "Yeah, well, me neither. But here we are. She seems upset, but there's nothing we can do about it."

They stood in silence for a moment. Finally, Iris broke it. "So, what are you going to do?"

Matthew shrugged again, his shoulders heavy with resignation. "I don't know. I guess nothing. Grace made it pretty clear she doesn't want anything to do with me."

"Maybe she's just upset. People say things they don't mean when they're mad."

Matthew glanced at her, a faint smile tugging at the corner of his mouth. "You sound like you've had some experience with that."

Iris rolled her eyes but couldn't help the small smile that crept onto her face. "Maybe."

They stood there a little longer, the awkwardness slowly fading.

"You know," Matthew said after a while, "I never understood why things between Grace and me got so complicated. It wasn't supposed to be like that."

"What do you mean?"

He sighed, kicking at a loose stone on the ground. "We were good together, at least I thought so. But it always felt like there was something… missing. Or maybe something in the way. I don't know. It's hard to explain."

Iris nodded slowly, understanding more than she wanted to admit. "Sometimes it's not about what's missing. Sometimes it's just not meant to be. Like a piece in a jigsaw puzzle. The wrong piece won't fit no matter how many times you try."

Matthew glanced at her, his eyes meeting hers for a brief, charged moment. "Maybe you're right. You're pretty smart for a kid."

And there it was. He saw her as a kid, but she was a woman. She didn't know what to say. "Well, I've got chores to finish," she said briskly, turning back toward the barn.

"Yeah, me too," Matthew replied, though he made no move to leave.

As Iris walked away, she couldn't help but glance over her shoulder. Matthew was still standing there, staring at nothing in particular, lost in thoughts she couldn't begin to guess. And for reasons she couldn't fully understand, that bothered her more than it should have.

CHAPTER 30

A couple of days on, Grace climbed into Daniel's buggy, the leather seat warm from the afternoon sun. Daniel gave her a quick smile as he flicked the reins, urging the horse forward. The rhythmic clatter of hooves on the dirt road filled the space between them, but Daniel noticed immediately that Grace was unusually quiet. Her gaze was fixed on the horizon, lips pressed into a thin line.

After a few moments, he glanced sideways at her, his brow furrowed with concern. "What is it?" he asked gently.

Grace hesitated, her fingers tightening slightly on the edge of her skirt. Finally, she sighed. "Someone's spreading rumors about me. Something about Ohio. But I've never even been there."

Daniel let out a sharp laugh, the sound startling against the quiet hum of the afternoon.

Grace turned to him, her eyes narrowing. "Do you think it's funny?"

SAMANTHA PRICE

He shook his head, though the smirk lingered on his face. "No, it's just..." He paused, as if choosing his words carefully, then shrugged. "I planted that seed."

Grace blinked, stunned. "What?"

Daniel kept his eyes on the road ahead, his tone casual. "I mentioned Ohio in passing to Wilma. Nothing specific, just enough to make her curious. I knew it would bother her and it would get her imagination going.'

"Why would you do that?"

Daniel's jaw tightened slightly, and for the first time, his confidence seemed to waver. "I didn't think it would get out of hand. I just... I thought it might make you look at me differently. Like maybe you'd turn to me if you felt like others were questioning you."

Grace stared at him, her breath coming in short, sharp bursts. "You wanted me to feel isolated? So I'd lean on you?"

He winced at her words, not denying them. "I didn't mean for it to hurt you. I just wanted—"

Grace cut him off, her voice trembling with fury. "You wanted to manipulate me. You wanted to control how I felt. That's not care, Daniel. That's cruel."

Daniel opened his mouth to respond, but she didn't give him the chance. She grabbed the reins from his hands, pulling the buggy to a sudden stop with a sharp tug. The horse neighed in protest, stomping its hooves against the dusty road.

Without another word, Grace climbed down from the buggy, her hands shaking. She didn't look back as she started walking, her footsteps firm and unyielding against the packed earth.

"Grace!" Daniel called after her, standing up in the buggy, his face pale. "Wait! Let me explain—the truth this time."

She didn't turn around. "There's nothing left to explain. I know exactly who you are now."

Daniel didn't hesitate. As soon as Grace stormed off, he leapt from the buggy and ran after her, the dust rising in small clouds beneath his hurried footsteps. "Grace!" he called, breathless. "Wait! Please, let me explain."

Grace spun around, her hands planted firmly on her hips, her eyes blazing with frustration. "Explain? Go ahead, Daniel. I'm listening."

He stopped a few steps away, catching his breath. "I just… I just wanted to stop those two old busybodies. They were trying to match me with you and someone else. Someone else was in the running, Grace, I'm sure of it. I think they were trying to find the best match for you, and I wanted you all to myself. Is that such a bad thing? That's why I did it and that's the truth. There, you know how I feel about you now."

Grace's eyes narrowed as she processed his words. She stared at him for a long moment, then, to his surprise, her expression softened. A small smile tugged at the corner of her lips. "You wanted me all to yourself? You feel that strongly about me?"

Daniel took a tentative step closer, his heart pounding. "Of course, I do. We've got something special, Grace, and I don't want to lose you to somebody else. Anybody else. I just want to see where this can go between the two of us."

Grace hesitated for a brief moment, then her smile grew, warm and genuine. She reached out and placed her hand in his, their fingers intertwining naturally.

Together, they walked back to the buggy. Daniel helped her up, his touch gentle, and soon they were settled side by side again. He flicked the reins, and the horse trotted forward, the tension between them melting away with each passing moment.

"So," Daniel said after a few minutes, his voice lighter, "how about we make the most of this day? I know a quiet spot by the river. It's peaceful, and the view's something else."

Grace nodded, her heart still racing, but this time for different reasons. "I'd like that."

The journey to the river was filled with easy conversation. They talked about simple things—memories from their childhood, favorite meals, the quirks of people they both knew.

Daniel guided the buggy to a stop beneath the shade of a large oak tree. The gentle sound of water flowing over rocks filled the air, mingling with the distant calls of birds. He helped Grace down from the buggy, and they spread a small blanket on the grass near the river's edge.

Daniel unpacked a simple picnic he'd brought—fresh bread, slices of cheese, crisp apples, and a small jar of honey. They sat side by side, their knees brushing occasionally, sending little sparks of warmth through Grace's chest.

As they ate, Daniel stole glances at her, noting the way the sunlight danced in her hair, the curve of her smile, the quiet way she listened when he spoke. He found himself talking more than usual, eager to fill the space with words, to share pieces of himself he rarely revealed.

After they finished eating, Grace leaned back on her elbows, gazing out at the water. "It's beautiful here," she murmured.

Daniel nodded. "It is. But not as beautiful as you."

Grace turned her head to look at him, her cheeks flushed with warmth. She laughed softly. "That's a little corny, Daniel."

He grinned, unbothered. "It's not corny if it's true. I meant what I said earlier, Grace. I do feel strongly about you. I've been trying to find the right words for a while now, but I guess I thought I had more time."

Grace tilted her head, studying him. "Why didn't you just tell me? Instead of... you know, planting rumors."

Daniel sighed, running a hand through his hair. "I was scared, I guess. Scared you'd choose someone else. Scared you wouldn't feel the same way. I thought if I made the competition disappear, I'd have a better chance."

Grace smiled gently, reaching over to squeeze his hand. "You didn't need to do all that, Daniel. You had a chance all along."

His heart swelled at her words. He turned his hand, lacing their fingers together again. "I'm glad to hear that."

After a while, they walked along the riverbank. The grass was cool beneath their feet. They talked more—about dreams for the future, places they'd like to visit, and the simple joys of life in their community.

At one point, they paused on a small wooden bridge that crossed a narrow part of the river. Daniel leaned against the railing, looking down at the water. "I've always liked this spot," he said quietly. "Feels like a place where you can be honest. No expectations, no judgments. Just... truth."

Grace joined him, resting her hands on the railing beside his. "Then tell me something honest."

He turned to face her, his expression serious. "I think I've been falling for you for a long time, Grace. I'm not talking this visit, I've liked you for the last few years, but seeing you with someone else there was nothing to be done."

Her breath caught slightly, but she didn't look away. "I never knew."

Slowly, Daniel reached out, brushing a loose strand of hair from her face. His hand lingered for a moment, cupping her cheek gently.

Grace leaned into his touch, her heart racing. She could see the sincerity in his eyes, the vulnerability he rarely showed. And in that moment, she realized she felt the same.

Daniel leaned in, his forehead resting gently against hers. "I don't want to rush you. I just needed you to know how I feel and that's what drove me to say that thing. I'm sorry if I hurt you. It was just a fun way for me to keep other men away."

Grace smiled softly, her eyes shining. "I'm glad you told me."

They stood like that for a long time, the world around them fading into the background. Eventually, as the sky darkened and the first stars appeared, they made their way back to the buggy.

The ride home was quiet, but it was a comfortable silence, filled with a new understanding between them. Daniel reached over once, taking her hand in his again, and Grace didn't let go until they arrived back.

As he helped her down from the buggy, he held onto her hand for a moment longer. "Thank you for today."

Grace smiled, her heart full. "Thank you for chasing after me."

Daniel chuckled softly. "I'd chase after you a thousand times if it meant we can be together."

With a final squeeze of his hand, Grace turned and walked toward her house, her heart lighter than it had been in a long time.

CHAPTER 31

Grace hadn't meant to tell Christina about Daniel's role in the Ohio rumor. The words had just tumbled out while they were washing dishes together, her excitement about Daniel's romantic gesture overwhelming her usual caution. "It was Daniel all along," she'd said, drying a plate with careful circles. "He started the rumor about Ohio because he wanted me for himself. Isn't that romantic?"

The crash of Christina's cup against the sink made Grace jump. Her birth mother turned, soap suds dripping from her hands, her face pale. "Did you say that Daniel started that rumor?"

"Yes, but—"

"Grace." Christina's voice was tight. "Do you understand what you're saying? He deliberately spread false stories about you? How is that romantic? It's anything but romantic. It's horrible."

"It wasn't like that," Grace protested, clutching the dish towel. "He just wanted—"

"To manipulate you? To damage your reputation?" Christina wiped her hands forcefully on her apron. "A man who would start rumors about a woman is not someone you should trust. You cannot see him again. I forbid it."

Grace felt her happiness crumbling. "But he did it because he loves me. He couldn't bear to see me with Matthew or any other man."

"That makes it worse!" Christina's voice rose. "Love doesn't justify spreading lies. Your reputation is everything in this community, Grace. Everything."

"What's going on in here?" Mark appeared in the doorway, drawn by Christina's raised voice.

Christina turned to her husband, her hands shaking slightly. "Grace just told me that Daniel was the one who started those rumors about something happening with Grace in Ohio."

Mark's usually gentle face hardened. "Is this true?"

"Yes, but you don't understand," Grace pleaded. "He knew Ada and Wilma were doing something like matchmaking us and they had another man they were thinking about for me too and he didn't want them to meddle anymore."

"Because he wanted you for himself," Christina cut in. "I heard. But that's not love, Grace. That's possession. That's manipulation."

Grace felt tears welling up. "He's not like that. You don't know him like I do. It wasn't like that at all. It was a good thing. He laughed when he told me about it."

"I know enough," Christina said firmly. "I'm going to write to your mother. She needs to know about this. She'll be in full agreement with me."

The words hit Grace like a physical blow. "No, please don't! Ma will never understand. She'll make me stop seeing him."

"Good," Christina replied, already moving to her writing desk. "That's exactly what needs to happen."

"But this could be the man I'll marry!" Grace's voice cracked. "Don't you understand? He's changed, he's grown. Everyone deserves a second chance. Just give him a chance to explain." Grace looked at Mark for help.

Mark stepped forward. "Grace, spreading rumors isn't just a mistake. It shows character. If he did this once, what's to stop him from doing it again? It is deceptive and I don't like it."

"He wouldn't," Grace insisted. "He loves me."

"Love doesn't excuse wrong behavior," Christina said, pulling out her writing paper. "I watched some people's reputation get ruined by malicious gossip. It followed them for years. I won't stand by and watch the same thing happen to you."

Grace turned to Mark, hoping for support. "Please, it was just a bit of fun to him. He didn't understand how serious it was."

"That's worse, isn't it?" Mark asked quietly. "Treating someone's reputation as a game?"

Grace felt the walls closing in. Everything that had seemed so romantic just minutes ago was being twisted into something ugly. She watched as Christina plucked a piece of paper and a pen from a drawer and sat at the kitchen table and started writing.

"I'm going to my room," Grace managed, her voice barely a whisper.

Neither Christina nor Mark stopped her as she hurried out of the room. She closed her door and sank onto her bed, tears flowing freely now. Why had she said anything? Everything had been perfect – she and Daniel were courting.

Now it was all falling apart. She could already imagine her mother's reaction to Christina's letter. Her mother, who valued honesty above all else, who had raised Grace to be truthful and direct. If only she could tell her mother in her own words. Christina would put a different slant on what really went on. Daniel was not being nasty.

Grace buried her face in her pillow, muffling her sobs. Through the wall she heard Christina and Mark's voices, discussing her future as if she were still a child.

She heard the twins at her door, and then Christina telling them to leave her alone.

Daniel was tender, thoughtful, respectful. Now people were thinking bad of him.

But how could she make Christina understand that? Her birth mother saw everything in black and white – right and wrong, truth and lies. She couldn't see the shades of gray, the way love could make people do foolish things.

Grace sat up, wiping her eyes thinking about the last time she'd seen Daniel. Would that future disappear now because of some careless words?

Her birth mother's letter would reach her adoptive mother soon, and then what?

She should have kept quiet. It wasn't even a rumor, it was a comment that he'd said to two meddling women. It had been said in fun.

But now everything was complicated. Christina was her

birth mother, and Grace desperately wanted to maintain their relationship. But Daniel... Daniel might be the only man she would ever love in this way.

Grace moved to her desk, pulling out her own paper and pen. She'd also write to her mother and explain everything. She'd post it first thing tomorrow before she started work.

Her perfect world was unraveling, all because she hadn't kept that one secret, that wasn't really a secret.

CHAPTER 32

Wilma stood by the stove, pouring steaming water into two mismatched mugs, the faint scent of chamomile mingling with the comforting aroma of fresh-baked bread. Iris sat at the kitchen table, her chin propped in her hand, her gaze distant.

"Here you go, dear," Wilma said warmly, setting a mug in front of Iris. The tea's gentle steam curled into the cool morning air. Wilma settled across from her, cradling her own mug.

Iris glanced at Wilma, her frustration bubbling to the surface. "I still can't believe Chess crashed into the shop and then set it on fire. It's like he can't help himself, always finding some way to mess things up. What did he have against that shop?"

Wilma gave a soft chuckle, her eyes kind but filled with a wisdom born from years of seeing life's ups and downs. "Oh, Iris, I know he's been a handful, but he's young. We all make mistakes. The important part is what we do after. He's offered to fix it, so that counts for something."

Iris huffed, staring into her tea as if it held the answers. "Offered, sure. But will he actually follow through? That's the real question."

"You'd be surprised what people can do when given a chance to make things right. Sometimes, it's the mistakes that shape us the most."

Iris nodded slowly. "Yeah well, he'll be shaped into something special with all the mistakes he's made." The familiar sound of hooves on gravel drew their attention. Iris sprang to her feet and looked out the window, her earlier mood lifting slightly. "It's Ada and Adaline."

Wilma's face lit up with a broad smile. "Wonderful."

They both headed to the door to greet them. "I've got something to share with you both!" Wilma announced as soon as she opened the front door.

Ada climbed down from the buggy carefully, her movements still showing traces of her recent injury. "Oh? What's that, Wilma?"

"Come sit and I'll tell you."

They settled onto the porch chairs. Romeo slipped out through the door and found a sunny spot near their feet, curling up contentedly. Wilma clasped her hands together, her eyes shining with anticipation. "I've decided what to do with the old shop. I'm going with Chess's idea to turn it into a mini guest house!"

Adaline's eyebrows shot up in surprise, her mouth opening slightly before she let out a delighted laugh. "A little guest house? That's wonderful."

Before Wilma could respond, Ada's brow furrowed slightly. "You didn't think to discuss that with me?"

Wilma chuckled lightly. "It just seems right. The foundation is still good, and we could use a place for visitors during harvest season."

Ada laughed, shaking her head. "Well, sometimes the best ideas come just like that. It sounds like a wonderful plan, Wilma."

They began discussing all the possibilities, their voices weaving together with enthusiasm.

"Imagine the cozy quilts on each bed," Adaline suggested, her hands gesturing animatedly. "And fresh flowers from the garden in little vases. It'll be like a home away from home for anyone who stays."

Iris leaned forward, her eyes sparkling with excitement. "We could even bake fresh bread for the guests! The smell alone would make them feel welcome."

Ada remained quiet for a moment, then gave a small nod. "I suppose it could be a good way to bring in some extra income for you, Wilma. And the building will be put to good use."

"There would be a small kitchen. Nothing fancy, but enough for guests to make their own breakfast if they want," Wilma said.

As they continued to talk, ideas flowed freely—curtains made from old linens, and a small rocking chair by the window.

"Of course," Wilma added, "None of this can start until after the harvest."

"Oh yes. That's coming up soon. I can barely wait," Adaline said.

The conversation drifted to harvest preparations, but then

they heard the distant clip-clop of another buggy approaching. Iris sat on the front steps, her chin resting on her knees, her eyes distant.

The slow, steady sound of the buggy drew closer. Not one of theirs. The rhythm of the hooves was unfamiliar, sharper, more deliberate. Romeo's ears perked up, and he raised his head to watch.

"Who's that?" Ada asked, squinting against the morning sun.

Wilma stood to get a better look, her hand shading her eyes. "I'm not sure. I can't recognize the driver. I don't think he's from around these parts."

The buggy rolled to a stop in front of the house. The driver climbed down slowly, his movements precise and deliberate. He pulled off his hat, revealing short, silver-streaked hair and a face tanned and angular. His clothes were plain and well-worn.

He took one step forward and called out. "There you are."

Ada sucked in a breath, and for a moment, even the crickets went silent. Romeo stood, fur bristling slightly, and moved under one of the chairs.

Iris stared at him. There was something about him — the way he stood, like he belonged there, like he'd been there before. Like he knew exactly where he was and why.

"There you are," he said again, his gaze locked onto Wilma's. "It's been a long time."

Wilma's hand found the porch railing, her fingers gripping it tight enough to turn her knuckles white. Her face was unreadable, but her eyes... her eyes were sharp as glass.

She stood and moved over to the top of the steps, drawing herself up straight. "What do you want?"

His reply came without hesitation. "Not much. Just what's owed to me."

~

THANK you for reading A Season of Secrets.

The next book - A Harvest of Hearts - is book 3 in the Amish Bonnet Sisters: Legacy of Faith series.

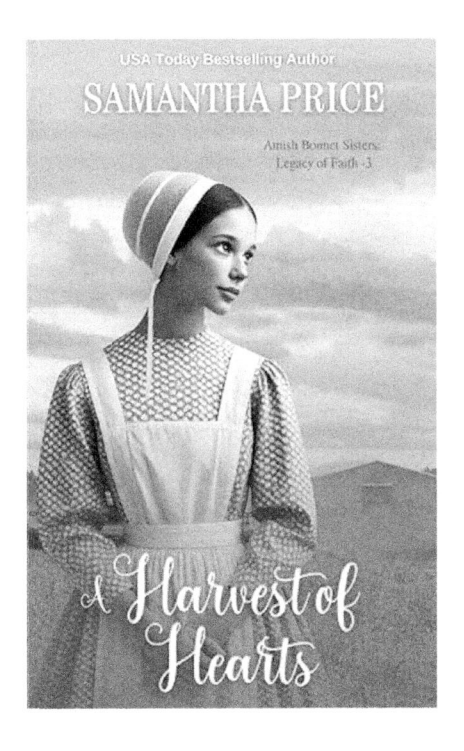

Just as the dust settles from one disaster, a mysterious stranger shows up at the Baker apple orchard—turning heads and stirring suspicion.

With the apple harvest about to begin, tensions rise. Chess shocks everyone with an unexpected act of redemption, Grace embraces a new love that might be too good to be true, and Iris wonders if her extended stay with Wilma is blessed or otherwise after a string of unsettling events.

A Harvest of Hearts

ALL SAMANTHA PRICE'S SERIES

For a downloadable/printable Series Reading Order of all Samantha Price's books, scan below, or head to: SamanthaPriceAuthor.com

Amish Maids Trilogy

Amish Love Blooms

Amish Bonnet Sisters: Legacy of Faith

ALL SAMANTHA PRICE'S SERIES

Drawn to Him: A Billionaire Rom Com Trilogy

Amish Misfits

The Amish Bonnet Sisters

Amish Women of Pleasant Valley

Ettie Smith Amish Mysteries

Amish Secret Widows' Society

Expectant Amish Widows

Seven Amish Bachelors

Amish Foster Girls

Amish Brides

Amish Romance Secrets

Amish Christmas Books

Amish Wedding Season

Shunned by the Amish

Amish Recipe Books

ABOUT SAMANTHA PRICE

Samantha Price is a USA Today bestselling and Kindle All Stars author of Amish romance books and cozy mysteries. She was raised Brethren and has a deep affinity for the Amish way of life, which she has explored extensively through over a decade of research. When she's not writing, Samantha enjoys cooking and spending time in nature, where she finds peace and inspiration for her stories.

www.SamanthaPriceAuthor.com

instagram.com/samanthapriceauthor
youtube.com/@samanthapriceauthor

RECIPE FOR RICH CHOCOLATE COOKIES

Amish Rich Chocolate Cookies

Servings: 24 cookies
Prep Time: 20 minutes
Bake Time: 10 minutes per batch

Ingredients:
- 1 cup (2 sticks) unsalted butter, softened
- 1 ¼ cups brown sugar, packed

RECIPE FOR RICH CHOCOLATE COOKIES

- ¾ cup granulated sugar
- 2 large eggs
- 2 teaspoons vanilla extract
- ½ cup unsweetened cocoa powder
- 4 oz semi-sweet baking chocolate, melted and cooled
- 2 ¼ cups all-purpose flour
- 1 teaspoon baking soda
- ½ teaspoon salt
- 1 ½ cups semi-sweet or dark chocolate chips

Instructions:

1. Preheat oven to 350°F (175°C). Line baking sheets with parchment paper.

2. In a large bowl, cream butter, brown sugar, and granulated sugar until light and fluffy.

3. Beat in the eggs, one at a time. Then add vanilla extract, cocoa powder, and melted chocolate. Mix until smooth.

4. In a separate bowl, whisk together flour, baking soda, and salt. Gradually add to the wet ingredients and mix just until combined.

5. Stir in the chocolate chips by hand.

6. Drop dough by rounded tablespoons onto prepared baking sheets, spacing them about 2 inches apart.

7. Bake for 10–12 minutes, or until the edges are set but the centers still look slightly soft. Do not over bake.

8. Let cool on the pan for 5 minutes before transferring to a wire rack to cool completely.

These cookies are even better the next day after the flavors deepen.

Find more Amish recipes in my spiral-bound Amish Bread, Cakes and Cookies recipe book.

Find all my Amish recipe books at:

https://samanthapriceauthor.com/collections/amish-cookbooks

Printed in Great Britain
by Amazon